THE NEW
ELVIS

The New Elvis

by

Wyborn Senna

The New Elvis
Copyright © 2014 by Marsha McLaughlin Radford
ISBN: 978-0-9785872-8-4

All rights reserved. No part of this publication may be reproduced, stored in a retrieval system, or transmitted electronically or mechanically. Neither photocopying nor recording are permitted without permission of the author.

All the characters, names, and events in this book are fictional. Any resemblance to actual people or occurrences is purely coincidental.

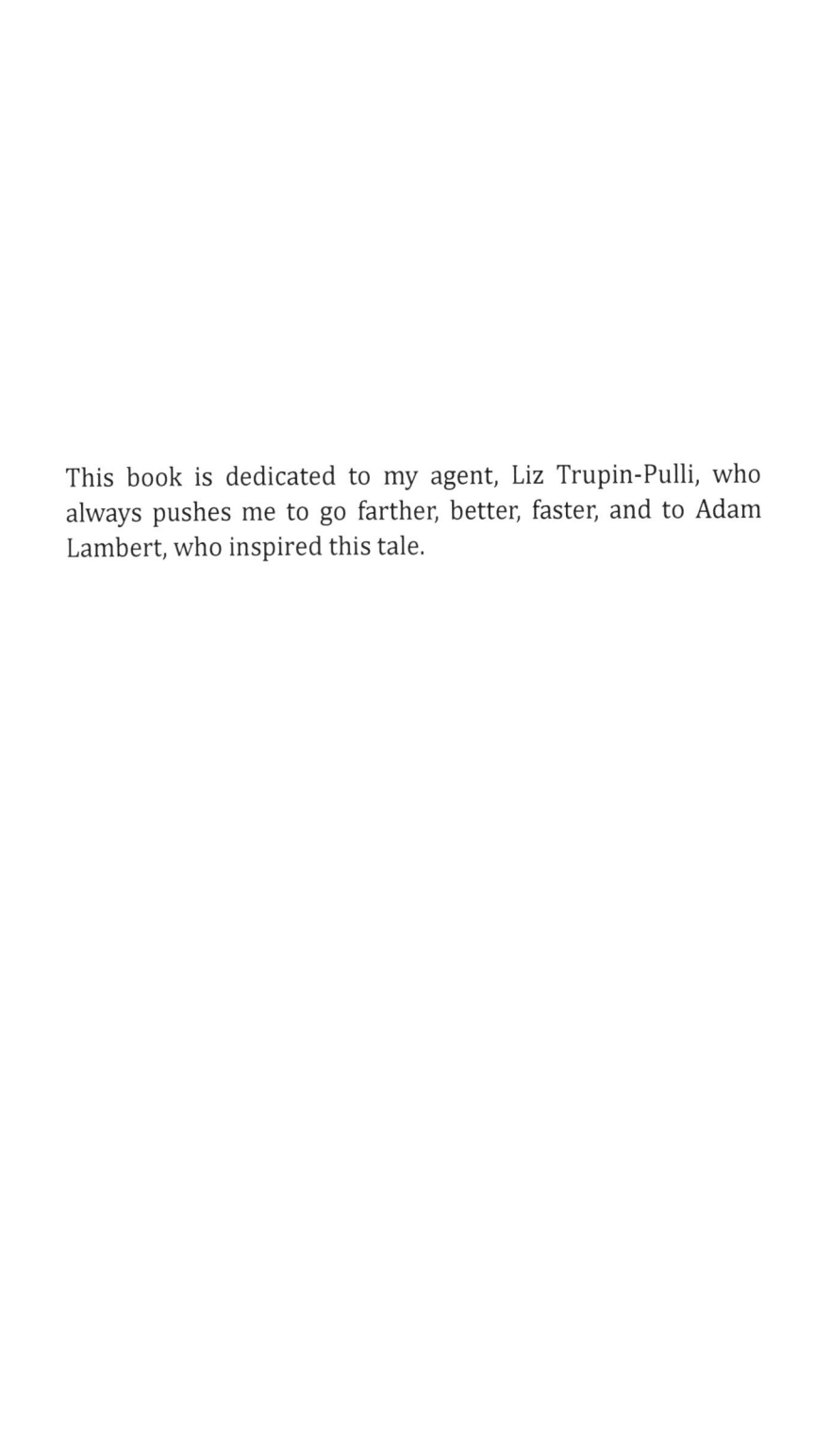

This book is dedicated to my agent, Liz Trupin-Pulli, who always pushes me to go farther, better, faster, and to Adam Lambert, who inspired this tale.

"Now, the finding of the father has to do with finding your own character and destiny. There's a notion that the character is inherited from the father, and the body and very often the mind from the mother. But it's your character that is the mystery, and your character is your destiny. So it is the discovery of your destiny that is symbolized by the father quest."

— Joseph Campbell, *The Power of Myth*

1

For some, Paradise is a resting place for meritable souls; for others, the heart of Sin City is a place to reinvent the future through pivotal deals, impulsive exploits, serendipitous encounters, and premeditated plans.

On the night of August 19, 1974, on the thirtieth floor of the Las Vegas Hilton, Elvis was feeling slightly tired but a little bit wired. He had just finished his second show, and it was two in the morning. Up in lavish suite 3000, he draped his scarf on a lamp, stripped off his concert whites, dropped his heavy belt, kicked off his shoes, and headed to the bathroom to take a shower. Twenty minutes later, he had on blue jeans and an embroidered patchwork jacket he wore as a shirt, unbuttoned from his neck to his chest. He came out to join Glen, James, Jerry, and Ronnie, grabbed a hot dog from a tray that had been set out, and left the room to make a phone call.

"Come back," Ronnie called.

Elvis ignored him. He dialed the front desk and explained what he wanted.

The clerk was stunned by his request but thought she could make it happen.

As though nothing out of the ordinary was about to transpire, Elvis returned to the gathering, grabbed a Pepsi, and cleared his throat. Glen began to play *Down In The Alley* on the piano, and Elvis sang, even though his voice was tired. The phone rang at three, and Elvis left the room to take the call.

"Do you need a car?"

"Sure. And make sure the driver knows where we're going."

Manny knew Vegas as well as his own reflection in the rearview mirror. He drove Elvis southbound down Paradise Road and took a right onto Harmon Avenue. Shortly before they reached the corner of Las Vegas Boulevard, he pulled over and stopped at the curb.

"See that building back there?"

Elvis lowered his window and peered into the darkness. Inset between a warehouse and a cluster of condominiums, the single-story medical office bore a discreet sign that read "Las Vegas Fertility Associates."

"Yep," Elvis told the driver.

They sat in companionable silence until a man in a white lab coat turned a light on and came to unlock the front door. Elvis jumped out of the limo and went to meet the doctor, whose name was Wendall Johns. They studied each other as they shook hands. To Elvis, Dr. Johns looked like a serious-minded professional whom he hoped regarded confidentiality as highly as the Pope revered the sacraments. That the doctor would don his white coat in the middle of the night to meet him seemed to be a good sign.

Dr. Johns had heard many stories about Elvis over the years and wondered how many of them were true. Tonight, the star's blue eyes were mere slits behind his gold-framed aviator-style glasses and his dark hair, swept back from his forehead, hung past his ears, nearly hiding his mutton-chop sideburns. He didn't appear as heavy as he looked on film, and his tan seemed faded. A diamond-studded gold Maltese cross hung from a chain around his neck, and his face looked wan in the moonlight.

The doctor ushered him inside and gave him a seat by his desk. "You sure you want to do this?"

Elvis stared at his vintage crystal opal and diamond pinkie ring like he was trying to recall where he'd bought it. He looked up suddenly. "Just give me a cup and a magazine," he said, straight-faced. "And I expect you to keep my identity a secret. You can provide prospective mothers with genetic information, but—"

Dr. Johns had heard about the various paternity cases filed against Elvis, and he wondered how many of the King's affairs had resulted in offspring. He also wondered about Elvis' drug use, erratic behavior, and lack of sexual interest in Priscilla after she became pregnant on their honeymoon in Palm Springs. Though he was not trained in psychiatry, Dr. Johns read plenty of psychoanalytic material, and it seemed that the virgin-whore dichotomy or Madonna-whore complex, wherein a virginal, young wife would begin to be seen as a mother and therefore not sexually attractive, fell in line with Elvis' intense devotion to Gladys. This also correlated to why Elvis seemed obsessed with virgins and why the star dated girls as young as age fourteen, even as he entered his twenties and thirties. They were girls, not mothers, so he could sexually desire them. If Elvis faced the obvious contradiction inherent in wanting children but desiring only virginal women, this was a bizarre way to fulfill his fantasy: he could have a child without compromising a woman's chastity.

"Little Lisa Marie isn't enough?"

The King leaned back in the chair and gave a halfhearted smile, his upper lip raised slightly but the sides of his mouth tense and tired. "Oh, sure, she's all that and a fleet of new Cadillacs. But now that I'm divorced from Priscilla, I'm not likely to father any more children, and if I did, they'd be unintentional. But this here has been well thought out. It's anonymous. It's clean. It's uncomplicated. And if you know anything about me, that's hard to come by. I can do it and when it's time to say howdy to the Good Lord and go catch up with Mama, I can leave, knowing I've left a little more of me behind."

"Another way of leaving your mark," the doctor acknowledged. He had heard this before from other sperm donors who had contemplated their mortality.

Elvis was as serious as a sober Sunday. "Make sure the woman are beautiful, if you can. It'd be nice to have some gorgeous kids. And, preferably, unmarried, just wanting to have a child in their life."

"Should they have good singing voices?"

Elvis shrugged. "Doesn't matter."

"Why don't we add virgin to the list while we're at it," Dr. Johns suggested, trying to sound jovial, but deadly serious.

Elvis sat up straighter in the chair and couldn't hide his genuine grin. It was clear to Dr. Johns that he loved the idea. "Why not? That sounds absolutely perfect. Add virgin to the list."

Dr. Johns wrote down "virgin" and thought, *Freud, you were one smart cookie.*

2

On the tenth anniversary of Elvis Presley's death, a plane crash at Michigan's Detroit Metropolitan Airport killed one hundred and fifty six people, one of them being Zella Stuart's childhood sweetheart, Glenn Enright.

In the summer of 1987, no one wore chastity rings vowing to remain pure until marriage, but Zella had a silver promise ring Glenn had given her their senior year at Grosse Pointe High. They had never made love, and Zella remained true to him even though she moved to Las Vegas to pursue her dream of becoming a magician with her own show on the strip, working in the interim as a cocktail waitress at the Flamingo until she got a permanent job as a magician's assistant and could begin her ascent up the show biz ladder.

Glenn planned to get an apartment near Zella's place in Vegas prior to their wedding. The night before their reunion, they couldn't stay off the phone. The last time they spoke was moments before Glenn's fatal flight, when they'd said they'd see each other soon.

Four months after his untimely death, Zella felt blue and well beyond her years. She walked down the strip and gazed at the Christmas lights and decorations that paled amidst the blaze of neon signs. She walked down Las Vegas Boulevard past the Aladdin and Little Caesar's Casino and turned onto Harmon, searching for the address listed on the business card she'd been given by her friend. The clinic sat between a warehouse and a cluster of condominiums, and there was nothing showy about it. The building sat far back from the street in the dimly lit lot, where a small sign identified it as Las Vegas Fertility Associates. Because it was the holiday season, a string of micro-lights framed the rectangular placard and cast tiny blue, red, green, and gold shadows across the shiny plastic letters.

Wearing a clean white lab coat, Dr. Wendall Johns turned on the light in the lobby and came to open the door for Zella. The linoleum entryway was crowded with potted poinsettias and a rosemary shrub decorated with lights and handmade clay ornaments.

Zella stopped at the tree and examined one of the pink ornaments, which bore a tiny handprint, the name "Melinda," and the year, "1985." Another pink one also bore a handprint no larger than a small plum, the name "Pearl," and the year "1984." A pale blue one with a handprint read "Abraham, 1981."

"Are these—?" she began.

"All our children," Dr. Johns said. He led her from the tree into the main office, where a desk and chairs were situated. A nativity scene complete with animals was arranged on a narrow table across the room, in front of a mirror with an ornate frame.

Zella could see her reflection and part of the desk, including Dr. Johns' forearm, which moved as he scribbled notes on paper laid atop a fresh folder. She smoothed back her straight dark hair and repositioned a clip that kept her bangs from falling into her eyes.

"Reason for wanting to conceive?"

Zella told him about Glenn's accident, how he had been the love of her life, how she would never meet anyone to match him, and that she wanted someone to love. "I tried a cat and then a dog. Then I took a roommate, Deb, who used to work with me, but now she teaches pre-kindergarten at The Meadows. She loves kids too."

"And you're how old?"

She pursed her lips and twisted the promise ring she still wore. "Twenty-two."

Dr. Johns studied her. Instead of shrinking under his scrutiny, she unclasped her pocketbook and removed a savings account passbook. She slid it across the desk so he could see its six-figure tally, thanks to the family life insurance Glenn's father shared, having considered his future daughter-in-law one of the clan.

Dr. Johns smiled. "I didn't know serving casino drinks paid that well."

"You wouldn't believe the tips some guys leave. But that's just a job. I'm the understudy for Max Maverick's assistant at the Riviera. After she leaves, I'll step in. Someday I want to have my own magic show on the strip."

The doctor resumed writing. "Your date of birth?"

"January 8, 1965."

Dr. Johns was startled. "Elvis' birthday."

Zella looked at the Mary and Joseph figurines. They gazed down at baby Jesus, who lay in his manger. "Funny you should mention Elvis. There's a rumor floating around the Flamingo that Elvis donated sperm here three years before he died."

"Where would someone get an idea like that?"

"One of the cooks is married to a woman who used to work here. Fay North?"

"Yes, Fay. Great bookkeeper. She retired last year."

"I've talked to her at parties," Zella said. "She's very colorful."

Dr. Johns laughed. "That she is. So, I need to know about your family."

"I have none," Zella told him. "I was an only child, raised by my mother. My dad had cancer and died when I was two. And she died last year. Heart attack."

Dr. Johns tapped his pen on the desk. No applicants had received Elvis' sperm in the past thirteen years because all of them had been sexually experienced. But here was Zella, wearing a purity band gifted to her by her late fiancé, as pretty as a pin-up girl and only twenty-two years young, looking to become a mother. And she shared her birthday with Elvis. Could it be a coincidence or were the heavens conspiring to fulfill the late King's wish?

"So, anything special you're looking for? Blue eyes and dark hair like yours?"

Zella smiled. "I'm a sucker for blue eyes."

3

Abercromby Chrome Shop was located near the beach on Ocean Avenue in Santa Monica, with a short unpaved road leading to its garage. Out back, you could see the Pacific, the surfers and their surfboards colorful daubs against the cerulean wash.

Calder Baillie had opened his shop to cater to the beachfront motorcycle crowd and hired Jarrod Lockhart when Jarrod was thirty-seven.

One day, Jarrod took his seven-year-old son Logan to work and showed him the piles of re-chromed bumpers that looked like silver canoes stacked against the corrugated walls. A smaller pile of unchromed bumpers lay stacked against a workbench where tools were scattered.

"So you make the old ones look shiny," Logan remarked, getting the picture.

"Yeah, but do you know how we do it?" Jarrod asked.

Logan shook his head and hiked up his jeans. He needed a belt but couldn't find one that morning under the piles of clothing in his bedroom.

"We etch it," his father explained.

Logan had an Etch-A-Sketch, but he no longer knew where it was. He once drew a house on it that was so narrow, its rooftop looked like the conical nose of a spaceship. Its front door was tall and narrow but there were no windows, which was strange, considering how much Logan loved them. "What do you draw with?"

Jarrod erupted with a thick, whiskey-laced, pack-a-day chuckle that nearly startled the boy, who seldom saw his dad in a good mood. "It's not a toy, it's a process. To etch a bumper, we dip it in sodium cyanide to prep the surface to accept a coat of something new."

Logan pictured a bumper wearing a dandy coat with brass buttons and wondered why it would need one unless it was cold out. Maybe these bumpers were being shipped to Alaska.

Jarrod pointed at a large vat with his dirty, scraped index finger. "See that red, goobery stuff over there? That gets crushed into a powder, and when you mix it, it's not red anymore, it's just smoky."

Logan shuffled his feet and gazed out the large picture window at the ocean.

A loud voice interrupted his reverie. "You're boring the boy, Jarrod."

Logan turned to see a skeleton of a man with tufts of brown hair patched in places on his scalp like clumps of grass. "This your son?" Out came a bony hand, and it pumped Logan's tender grip with a ferocity that frightened the boy.

"I'm Mr. Baillie," he said, "and I know who you are because your dad works extra hard to make sure you and your mom have everything you need. Especially your mom." Calder's glance slid sideways and he winked at Jarrod. "Say you've got a skull and crossbones, right? Not a real one, but a metal one you want to mount on top of the gas tank, but you want it fancy. You heat up sodium cyanide to one-hundred-and-eighty degrees and you dip the skull and crossbones in, and the metal gets etched, which means the structure is changed so other metals will stick to it. Then you take that skull and crossbones to another vat full of something shiny like melted bronze or chrome or copper or silver, and you dip it in and take it out, and you've got a shiny skull and crossbones."

Logan did his best to follow what Mr. Baillie said, but it was fairly complicated.

Jarrod spoke up. "Say you've got a piggy bank full of nickels. You could melt them down, put an etched object into the melted nickels, and the object would have a shiny coating of melted nickels."

"Why would I want to melt my nickels?"

The men laughed at that and allowed Logan to wander away so they could talk.

"You gonna meet Skeet tonight?" Calder asked.

Jarrod answered quietly, quickly. "Yeah, at eight."

"Make sure you count it before you leave."

Jarrod nodded and glanced over at Logan. Abercromby Chrome was not only in the business of re-chroming bumpers, it made the meat of its money from a tidy little meth lab Calder ran in the basement of the shop. Chemicals and chrome shops went together like sugar and bakeries. No one suspected that large orders for chemicals used to produce his product were used for anything but legitimate reasons, and the extra income insured the longevity of not only the establishment but of Jarrod's marriage to Ramona, a hoarder who spent most of her husband's paycheck as soon as he brought it home. Without drug deals on the side, there would be nothing to put aside for any of life's little emergencies.

With this as his rationalization, Jarrod made sure most of Santa Monica had all the ice it needed, even if he wasn't a tweaker himself.

4

Two things happened to Zella on her twenty-third birthday in 1988 that would change her life forever. First, she discovered she was pregnant, and second, she met Eugene Wyatt, a real estate agent from Los Angeles. Twenty years her senior, Eugene looked exactly like she imagined Glenn might in his forties, with a touch of gray in his dark brown hair, crow's feet at the corner of his azurite eyes, and a slight gut pooching out over his belt. He was alone, seated at the Munster nickel slots three stools down from an old lady who had chain-smoked her way through most of a pack of Eve Lights.

He wanted a vodka tonic, which was Glenn's drink, and asked for olives on the side. When Zella delivered his complimentary drink and he tipped her five dollars, she couldn't help herself. She noticed he did not wear a wedding band, and lingered, hoping to find out more about him. He introduced himself and told her he was there for a realtors' conference and would be in town till Tuesday. It was atypical of Zella to accept dates with strangers, but she felt lightheaded when she looked at him and couldn't say no.

She wrote her home phone number on a cocktail napkin, which he tucked into the pocket of his blazer. Zella had Mondays off. Eugene called at noon and they met at one o'clock at the entrance to the Paradise Garden buffet at the hotel. It was a gorgeous day, and the large windows made them feel as though they were in a terrarium, looking out at the wildlife, waterfalls, and palms that filled the preserve.

Eugene laughed. "Are they watching us or are we watching them?"

"I think it's a little of both," Zella decided. Dressed in a wide-brimmed hat and a flouncy dress, she felt carefree, impulsive, and ravenous, eager to take full advantage of the salad bar before adding snow crab legs, prime rib, glazed duck, and mussels to her plate. Eugene concentrated on sautéed clams and fried chicken, with only a smattering of salad and veggies to round out his meal. After ice cream sundaes, they pushed back their chairs and gazed outside at the flamboyant flamingos and parleying penguins in contented silence.

"I love a woman who can eat as much as I can," Eugene noted.

"I love a man who doesn't care how much a woman eats," she replied.

They discussed Bugsy Siegel's affiliation with the Flamingo and how he named it after his girlfriend Virginia "Flamingo" Hill, who had long, slender legs. Zella recounted a story about the hotel and casino's grand opening the day after Christmas in 1946, when Jimmy Durante, Lana Turner, Clark Gable, and Joan Crawford danced to the music of Xavier Cugat's band. After three hours melted away, it was time to part, but they couldn't. Zella followed Eugene up to his room and sat on his king-sized bed.

She was perfectly candid with him and admitted she was still a virgin, holding out her left hand and showing him the promise ring she still wore. "Glenn and I were waiting till marriage."

Eugene sat down at the secretary desk. "I'm sorry you lost him."

Zella looked thoughtful. "It's strange, but the only time he crossed my mind today was when I realized again how much you look like him."

Eugene sounded rueful. "An older him."

"True," she laughed. "But still..."

"We're bound to be a little different, he and I."

"Well," Zella said. "I'll just have to find out what makes you *you*."

"Sounds good." Eugene moved from the desk to the bed. He took Zella in his arms and kissed her, tossing her hat toward the pillows, running his fingers through her long, dark hair.

"Have you ever been married?" Zella asked.

"Yes, and divorced. My ex-wife remarried and moved to Sherman Oaks and seems much happier now. We met in high school and married young. No kids."

"Glenn and I met in high school."

Eugene rested his forehead against hers. "You've got to stop talking about him."

Her words were barely louder than a murmur. "Make me forget."

5

The first hint Logan had that his father was involved in something shady came on a warm spring day when Logan was eight and his dad picked him up from school before driving to Culver City. There, behind a small bookstore on Overland Avenue, he watched from the passenger seat as his dad got out of his beloved vintage Chevelle SS 396, its shiny black paint job polished to a high sheen, and approached a small gray car with darkened windows.

A man in the other car lowered the passenger window, and an envelope was passed from a gloved hand to his father. Then Jarrod reached inside his pocket for a small packet, which the gloved hand accepted. The window stayed open a crack, but the men did not speak. Jarrod waited, ran a cut and bandaged hand back through his dark hair, and seemed to examine his Levi's jacket for lack of anything more useful to do.

Finally the window closed and Jarrod nodded. The car jerked into reverse and then forward, careening out of the parking lot, tires squealing. Jarrod turned and walked back to the car. Logan thought he had never seen his father look wearier. His clothes were dirty from work, and there was a new crack in the leather of his work boots, which, when new, seemed indestructible, with steel toes and soles as thick as sponges.

As swiftly as the dark car had vanished, a new car rushed into the parking lot, this one a sickly green with white scrape marks along its side. Before the vehicle stopped, a tatted man in a torn undershirt and baggy pants leapt out of the back seat. He ran up to Jarrod and stood so close, their faces were inches apart.

"What you doing here, man?" The guy was impossibly loud.

Jarrod stepped back. "Just—" He glanced backward toward the car, nervous, and Logan instinctively crouched down below the dashboard.

"You have no business here, okay? You don't deal in Culver. Got it?"

Jarrod was quiet. Baillie told him the transaction would be hassle free, but he'd been wrong before. If he made any moves or said anything, this guy was prepared to take it to the next level.

"Tell Baillie to keep it in his own backyard. If I see you around here again, I'll kill your wife and kid first, then come after you and tell you how it all went down."

Jarrod flashed another glance toward the car and didn't see Logan.

The man wiped a hand across his brow, then stuck his hand into his pants and pulled out a revolver. "Yeah, you think I didn't notice the boy? What kind of dad brings his kid to a drop? Asshole. So, what are you supposed to do?"

Jarrod spoke quietly. "Stay out of Culver City."

"That's right, Pops."

Close enough to kiss Jarrod, the man spit on him, daring him to start something, but Jarrod refused. The man went back to his car, jumped in, closed the passenger door, and gave a sign to the driver. They peeled out of the lot. It was only then that Logan sat up again and saw his father, who had crumpled to his knees in the gravel.

6

Zella and Eugene Wyatt fell in love, were married at Wee Kirk of the Heather in Las Vegas in March of 1988, and settled into his home in the Beverly Hills flatlands after honeymooning in Barbados. That Zella had been a virgin yet was pregnant courtesy of Dr. Johns' sperm bank was not something they discussed with friends and neighbors. When Zella's water broke the morning of October third, Eugene rushed her to Cedars-Sinai, and Ryan Bryan Wyatt, situated in the breach position with his legs crossed Indian style, was delivered at three that afternoon via Caesarean section.

Growing up amidst luxury in Beverly Hills, little Ryan attended Page Private School as soon as he turned five, entering pre-kindergarten at the same time his neighbor, little Beatrice Edwin, did. Beatrice loved playing at Ryan's house because Zella had decorated the Spanish courtyard style home in bright colors that would later, when *SpongeBob Squarepants* debuted on television, remind everyone of Bikini Bottom. Rooms were painted plum, mottled with lighter purple; lime, mottled with evergreen; and turquoise, mottled with light blue. There were Tiki carvings and aquariums, a modern pop art Tiki bar with stools, retro sectional sofas and low-slung chairs, boomerang-shaped lamps, glass tables, shag wall-to-wall carpeting, stone and brick walls, and freestanding globe-shaped fireplaces. There was an ocean mural in Ryan's bedroom, complete with fishermen, ships, jumping porpoises, whales, and mermaids. Even his toys were kept in fishing nets suspended from ceiling hooks and adorned with starfish, shells, and plastic lobsters. Outside, in the courtyard, there was a sandbox, slide, swings, a pond, and a pool frequented by Nana, the family's black Newfoundland, named after the kind-hearted canine in J. M. Barrie's *Peter Pan*.

After kindergarten one day, Bea and Ryan were playing in his room together when Zella heard music. Their teacher, Richard Prescott, was known to love musicals, and he enjoyed Rodgers and Hammerstein most of all, oftentimes giving recordings of R&H show tunes to the kids to take home. Ryan was well versed at using his plastic cassette player, which had buttons for stop, start, play, fast-forward, and rewind marked with pictures. Mr. Prescott had given him a tape of *Oklahoma,* and he and Bea were standing in front of his mirror, singing *People Will Say We're In Love.*

Zella snuck down the hallway, marveling that the kids had memorized the lyrics.

Little Bea was singing to Ryan, who wore a jaunty wool fedora and an oversized blue blazer that draped down to the floor, both borrowed from his father's closet. When Bea was done with her verse, Ryan sang the next one to her.

Zella gasped. Ryan's voice was in tune and as clear as a bell. Backing up to the hall closet, she retrieved the video camera and pressed the record button as she crept back to his room. Noticing his mother's reflection in the mirror, Ryan turned and approached her, getting down on his knees, continuing to sing, not missing a beat. When the song ended, he rose from the floor and pushed the off button on the cassette player.

Bea beamed at Ryan's mom. "So, Mrs. Wyatt, are we ready for Broadway?"

Zella sat down on the turquoise rug. "Come here and see for yourself."

They crowded onto her lap as she hit rewind so they could watch the video play back in the viewfinder. When the recording was done, Bea and Ryan applauded.

Though Zella shared the tape with her husband, Eugene didn't witness Ryan's talent firsthand until three years later, when he came home and heard singing coming from his son's room. Approaching the closed door, he listened as Ryan sang *A Little Less Conversation* from *Live A Little, Love A Little*, an Elvis Presley movie from 1968.

7

Logan woke up in the corner of his room with swollen glands, and he dreaded telling his mother, because he knew she would keep him home from school.

Ramona Lockhart had started hoarding since her mother died five years earlier, and as the years passed, their residence became less of a home and more of a garbage dump. Jarrod was at his wit's end and chose to handle the situation by working long hours at Abercromby's and on the streets as a dealer for Calder's meth. In his father's absence, Logan, an only child, was left to face long hours at home alone with Ramona. He found himself parenting her, trying to curb her online shopping and frequent trips to local thrift stores by finding petty distractions to pull her off her destructive course.

This morning, he picked his way down the hallway through bags of still-tagged, never-worn clothing, purses, and shoes. He found Ramona in a spare room, where she kept a record player and a collection of albums scattered atop boxes stacked on chairs and tables. She was nearly in a trance, listening to The Andrews Sisters singing *Sincerely* in distinctive three-part harmony.

Logan had trouble getting to her and nearly tripped. He ended up falling in front of her, into in a pile of used, folded, recyclable plastic bags she refused to discard.

Over three-hundred-and-fifty pounds, Ramona used a walker for support, clinging to walls and furniture to navigate piles of debris. At twenty-nine, she looked two decades older, with strikes of gray throughout her knee-length, straight dark hair, which took two hours daily to wash and braid. Wrinkles creased her forehead, eyes, and mouth. She smoked not one but three packs of Camels every twenty-four hours, leaving overflowing ashtrays in her wake whenever she moved from one room for the next.

"*Mas música*," she cried out in Spanish, lapsing into her mother's native language.

More music. Logan tugged at the collar of the t-shirt he'd slept in and kept his distance lest she pull him into a smothering bear hug. She loved her only boy, even if she didn't know how to take care of him.

"I'm sick. It feels like I swallowed eggs."

"Your glands! Swollen again?"

He nodded.

She struggled to get up from the cushioned chair, but he put out his hand in protest. "I'm just going to sleep."

"What about breakfast?"

Logan knew what was in the kitchen: dirty dishes piled on countertops, unwashed pots in the sink, rotten food in the refrigerator, ice-encrusted artifacts in the freezer, and no place to sit down because the dining table and chairs were buried in clutter.

"It's okay."

He picked his way out of the room and made his way back to his bedroom.

He didn't have a bed, so he usually formed a pile of clothing—some clean, some not—in the corner and crawled on top, pulling something weighty—usually a coat—over his frail frame so he could stay warm. For a pillow, he used a bolt of quilted fabric his mother bought at The Salvation Army down the street. It didn't matter to him if he didn't eat that day. He had gone hungry before rather than eat something spoiled that had been unrefrigerated too long. If he were lucky, Ramona would muster up the energy to get her walker in gear and head to McDonald's for some fast food. And if her conscience rumbled louder than her stomach, maybe she would be consider saving half a bite for him.

8

Ryan Wyatt got his first guitar the Christmas he turned ten and wrote his first song two days shy of his eleventh birthday in the privacy of his bedroom. The décor hadn't changed much as he got older, save for the addition of an ivory coin bank shaped like a skull that sat on his desk, watching his pen move across the pages of his early American history notebook, where he dutifully entered multiple choice answers to questions from his textbook on the U.S. Constitution and the Bill of Rights.

The words running across the page...*blah blah blah*...were nudged by strings of new ones. *All my worries used to be...blah blah blah...where to go and who to see...blah blah blah...now I'm older, lookin' around...blah blah blah...wondering about the new girl in town.* Ryan threw down his pen and ran to his bed, where his Les Paul sat in its open, velour-lined case. *Oh, she's blonde, and she's boogie, wanna call her my shoogie, with hair down to there and a thousand-yard stare, she's a cinnamon heart of a cutie.*

An electric thrill raced down Ryan's spine. He sprinted back to his desk, wrote two more verses to run against the chorus, and returned to his bed to bang out the melody. Inspiration struck swiftly and the payoff rolled out faster than a greyhound on race day. He'd been barely able to write down one line before another tumbled out and rendered him deliriously happy. He ran over to the mirror to make sure he hadn't been transported to another realm. His handsome young features—clear blue eyes, thick dark hair, lopsided grin, and strong jaw—were reflected back at him. He was the same boy in the same house, with the same guitar, yet he felt reborn and more alive than ever.

The word came to him—*purpose*—and it swam around in his mind until it merged with the porpoises on his underwater mural, and he laughed aloud with pleasure.

9

An ordinary chain-link fence separated Jarrod and Ramona Lockhart's property from the family that lived behind them, but it didn't stop Logan from trying to make friends with the boy who lived there, Fred Henn.

When summer arrived and Fred's eleventh birthday loomed, Kara Henn sent out invitations to the boys in Fred's class for a pool party in their backyard, complete with pizza, sodas, cake, and a clown. Not being in Fred's class, Logan wasn't invited, but the morning they began hanging crepe streamers outside, Ted Henn took pity on the boy and issued him an invitation.

Excited, Logan searched for his swim trunks in the piles of clothing that had formed like haystacks throughout his room. His mother was in the kitchen, burning bacon and eggs for his father, who hadn't found an adequate excuse to escape her rare offer to push all the trash aside and try to cook a meal.

Flipping through channels on the television positioned across from the cluttered kitchen table, Jarrod settled on NBC Sports and lit a cigarette. He was in his undershirt and shorts and needed a shower, but it was Saturday and Abercromby's was closed until noon because Calder Baillie needed to fill double his usual meth orders.

Ramona was giddy with excitement. She had found her frying pan in a cupboard filled with old glass jars her mother had used for preserves. Once she cleared off the stove, she could make a late breakfast, and maybe, if Jarrod showed interest, they could find time to be alone.

The bacon and eggs were beginning to blacken as smoke filled the kitchen.

Jarrod jumped out of his seat. "Jesus, woman! What the hell are you doing?"

"I thought you liked your bacon crisp."

"Yeah, but not my nose hair!"

Logan couldn't find his swimsuit, so he put on a pair of shorts and wandered outside. He had dug a hole directly into the neighbors' backyard, so he crawled under the fence and looked up at the treehouse in the oak that grew along the property line, where Logan spent many a night whenever his parents argued. He sat down and watched as a pair of Fred's classmates showed up and placed gifts on the picnic table.

Kara came out with a stack of plastic cups and a pitcher of lemonade. "Hi, boys. Fred is inside. I'll tell him you're here. You can put your towels over there." She indicated another table near a sandbox filled with Tonka trucks.

"Cool," the taller one, named Eben, said.

The boys stripped off their jeans and shirts to reveal swimming trunks.

Wearing a pair of board shorts, Fred came out of the house and pointed at the pool. "Jump in, guys."

They did, and soon Fred joined them. Within a half hour, a dozen more boys arrived. Logan worked up the courage to try the pool. He stepped into the shallow end and sat down on the steps. The water was up to his chest.

Ramona's voice was so loud she could be heard in the Henns' yard. "You're not going anywhere!"

Jarrod was just as loud, just as caustic. "The hell I'm not!"

Logan slid down the steps of the pool and sank down into the water. The argument escalated, and Logan reddened, certain someone would notice him. Kara came out with more lemonade and stopped beside her husband, who was setting up lawn chairs.

"Are they at it again?" Ted's eyes darted around the yard. He had invited Logan to the party but didn't see him anywhere.

Logan was ashamed. It hadn't always been like this. He shut his eyes and drifted back to a time when MawMaw was still alive and his mother was happy. MawMaw had her own room, and it was the only place in the house that was kept clean and tidy. Even now, her belongings remained in the drawers and closet, as though she were still alive. Occasionally, Logan escaped to her room to be alone in the dark and inhale the scent of lavender sachets she kept buried among her stockings. The only clutter back then was Ramona's ever-increasing stack of Elvis Presley albums, which Ramona and MawMaw listened to as they played cards at the dining room table. Logan remembered them all—the one of Elvis in his tropical shirt and the swirly lettering of the words "Blue Hawaii," the black and white one that said "Elvis" in red along the left-hand side of the cover and "Presley" in green along the bottom, and the one where golden records were hung like ornaments, with Elvis' face on one of them. The golden records one had songs like *Hound Dog, All Shook Up, Heartbreak Hotel*, and *Jailhouse Rock* on it, and it was just about MawMaw and Ramona's favorite.

Logan was only five when MawMaw died, and sometimes he was certain his mother had died with her. At least he knew her heart had. In the months following her mother's passing, Ramona dedicated herself to buying useless items, cluttering up every square inch of the house but leaving MawMaw's shrine intact. He wanted to go back to the days of Elvis, when both of the ladies would sit at the table, drinking gin and tonics, smoking cigarettes, playing cards, gossiping like schoolgirls. Their laughter and the clinking of ice in their glasses complemented the music they listened to, and now that it was gone, all that was left in the house was the seething resentment between his parents.

Ramona was still screaming now, but Jarrod hadn't left.

Kara restacked the plastic cups on the table. "Isn't there something we can do?"

Finally, one of the boys noticed Logan pressed against the side of the pool, in the shallow end. "Hey, Lockhart, don't your parents ever shut up?"

A few boys made their way to the shallow end and one of them grabbed him. "Don't you ever get sick and tired of listening to them argue?"

One of the boys laughed and jumped on Logan, pushing him down, holding him under the water.

"Maybe they're arguing about him. Maybe they're sorry they had him. Maybe things would be better if he were dead."

Underwater, Logan held his breath for as long as he could. Then he started to feel dizzy. Oblivious of the fact that a boy had shouted Logan's name and that he was in the pool, Kara was still talking to Ted. "That poor boy. Someone should get him away from those people."

"Hey, cut it out, guys!" Fred pushed his friends out of the way and dragged Logan to the surface.

Logan sputtered and coughed.

Kara finally noticed him. "Oh, my God!"

Fred slapped Logan on the back, trying to clear his lungs. "You okay, dude?"

The boys who had been pushed away muttered to themselves and moved to the deep end. Logan wished Fred a happy birthday and got out of the pool. Kara noticed he didn't have a towel, so she brought over one of hers and dried him off.

"It's rough at home, isn't it, Logan?"

Logan shook his head, trying to be tough.

Kara's words were hesitant. "If you ever need anything..."

"Thanks, Mrs. Henn. I'll be okay."

Now dry, Logan walked back to the fence and crawled under it. He turned back, wanting to thank Mr. Henn for inviting him, but no one was watching.

10

Ryan's voice was angelically high and sweet. Puberty hadn't raised a pimple, but he already loved music and girls, and of all the girls in the world, little Beatrice Edwin ranked higher on his best-loved list than chocolate in his milk, frosting on his cake, sleeping in on Saturdays, baseball with his buddies, and his favorite song—*Jailhouse Rock*—all rolled into one. Most of all, he loved to spend time with her in her bedroom, decorated with Disney princesses and an ever-increasing number of wall clocks. Right after Thanksgiving, in early December, they lay on the floor in her frilly room, staring at a new cuckoo clock she'd placed on the wall above her dresser, waiting for four p.m. sharp so they could watch the cheery bird pop out.

Ryan had brought his guitar over and wanted to cook up a new song for the Christmas talent show at Page. *Cuckoo...hours... minutes...seconds...* He thought maybe something about Bea's growing obsession with clocks would inspire him.

"Talk about time," he prompted.

"Time is all we've got." She raised her butt and tried to lift her legs back over her head, being goofy. She was dressed in leggings and a black top with tiny rosettes.

"I read *Barlett's Quotations* for inspiration, but those dead guys all say the same things. Don't waste time, seize the moment, one day at a time, and time changes everything."

Finally, the blue wooden cuckoo bird popped out of his door and cuckooed four times. Bea jumped up. "Let's stroll the neighborhood."

She ran to her closet, pulled a heavy sweatshirt off a hanger, and struggled to tug it over her tangle of sandy blonde curls.

Ryan got up and reached for his jacket. "I like flower imagery, how time unfolds like petals."

Bea grabbed her brush and ran it through her hair. "Me too."

Ryan scanned the room while buttoning his jacket. "You have about a dozen clocks now. Why?"

Bea placed her brush back on top of her vanity next to her collection of empty perfume bottles she'd gathered from neighborhood trashcans and cleaned. She only liked ones she considered pretty, and over the past three years, she'd found eight. "Come on. We have to be back in time for dinner."

Ryan wanted an answer, so he sat on the edge of her canopied bed and waited.

Restless, Bea paced as she looked around her room. "I got my first clock from my dad when he came back from Amsterdam four years ago. It's that one." She pointed to a small silver clock on her dresser. "I thought he would be gone forever, but so much was happening at school, it felt like he was only gone a day or two before he was back. So I started thinking about time and how it goes quickly sometimes, especially when you're happy, and how it just about kills you by dragging along when you're not. I like the perception of it and our inability to stop it. It's all we have. It's relentless, and we have to make the most of it."

"Relentless," Ryan reiterated. "And we have to make the most of it."

Bea was emphatic. "We do."

"So let's go and see how the neighbors decorated their homes for the holidays."

"Let's," she agreed, grabbing his hand, pulling him toward the door.

11

The night Manny drove Elvis southbound on Paradise Road, took a right onto Harmon and stopped at the curb before they reached the corner of Las Vegas Boulevard, Ramona Johns was smoking a cigarette on the porch of the condo unit she shared with her mother and her brother Wendall. The front door to Wendall's practice, Las Vegas Fertility Associates, was within shouting distance, and it was clear to her that her brother, the good doctor, was about to meet a very special client, because limousines seldom stopped there.

Ramona was too far away to hear the muffled exchange between the man and the driver, who spoke with him before the man got out and shut the door on the passenger side facing the sidewalk. Wendall turned on the light in his office and disappeared from Ramona's view as he headed down the hallway to the front door, then reappeared to unlock the entrance. He stepped halfway out and waved.

Ramona took a deep drag on her cigarette and moved closer. She bumped the card table her ashtray was stationed on, and red and white plastic chips from an earlier card game with MawMaw slid across the laminated surface of the table and splattered onto the second story porch. The client did not look up, and Ramona watched him walk. With every step he took, amazement and increasing recognition blossomed in her heart until it fluttered as rapidly as a hummingbird's wings. She knew, from his trademark rings to his aquiline nose, from his full lips to his glistening black hair that shone in the dim security lights along the side of the condominium complex that Elvis was in the parking lot. Her squeal overlapped with her brother's question, so she never heard what Wendall asked him. Wendall locked the front door after letting him in, and the men disappeared down the hallway. By the time they reappeared in Wendall's office, the doctor went to the window and drew the shades.

Ramona finished her cigarette and picked up the plastic poker chips, returning them to the wooden carousel on the table. Then she went inside the three-bedroom condo to get her Polaroid camera, buried beneath her oversized lingerie in the bottom drawer of her bureau. The door to MawMaw's bedroom was closed; Ramona dared not wake her mother, who was generally good-natured except when being disturbed from a sound slumber. She returned to the porch and sat down heavily on one of the heavy-duty folding chairs before she dumped her full ashtray over the balcony railing and lit a fresh cigarette.

By the time she was on the eighth cigarette of her wait, her eyes flew open. Perfectly balanced upright between the index and middle fingers of her right hand resting on the card table, her cigarette had burned down to an inch of ash and stopped at the filter. Wendall's office building was now completely dark, and the limousine parked by the curb was gone.

12

The school was decorated with holiday lights shaped like chili peppers, and the pre-show buffet in the dining hall was authentic Mexican, with celebrity chef Judd Smith running a kitchen filled with his students.

While most parents had arrived early with their kids to eat beforehand, Gene had a late meeting, so he and Zella planned only to attend the show at eight. Glad for the extra practice time before curtain, Ryan sat in a corner of the dance classroom on a foam mat and scrutinized his reflection in the wall of mirrors as he pulled out his guitar. Bea promised to meet him there at seven-thirty, and it was now seven-fifteen.

Aretha Franklin got respect, and Gaye wished it would rain, Presley had amazing grace, and Sam Cooke promised change. Lennon smoked Norwegian wood, Ray Charles—What'd I Say, Dylan dreamt of a drifter's escape, and Redding loved the bay. Stevie Wonder lit a roaring fire, James Brown was a prisoner of love, Paul McCartney could easily carry that weight, Little Richard drew strength from above. A wop bop a loo mop a lop bam boom, time is fast a-fleeting while we're sitting in this room, a wop bop a loo mop, don't like a thing, a wop bop a loo mop, go and jump for that ring.

Roy Orbison heard distant drums, Green had a broken heart, Robert Plant knew cities don't cry, with Jagger alone from the start. Tina Turner was an acid queen and Freddie the great pretender, Marley knew three little birds, and Smokey sang songs of surrender. Johnny Cash was the man in black, Etta James would rather go blind, Bowie mulled over life on Mars, Van Morrison mystic eyes. A wop bop a loo mop a lop bam boom, time is quickly ticking, go and put your lens on zoom, a wop bop a loo mop, don't win spit, a wop bop a loo mop, try again and never quit.

Ryan rang through the song once and glanced at his watch. Three minutes had passed. He repeated the song twice more and then put his guitar back into its case. Closing his eyes, he imagined the audience cheering for him as he finished his original composition. He would graduate to cool rocker status and people would know his name.

He straightened the sleeves on his jacket and shook out his pant legs. Maybe Bea misheard him and thought they were meeting someplace else. Wandering down the hallways, he checked the classrooms and listened at the girls' bathroom door for any activity within. The only noise resonating throughout the building emanated from the cafeteria. Most people had finished their meals, but in the far corner of the room near the fire exit, three boys from his homeroom were pelting each other with hard taco shells.

It was almost eight. Ryan hurried toward the auditorium, passing a friend from math class who wished him good luck. Then he turned the corner, where the choir and band rooms were, and finally found Bea. She was leaning against the wall near the water fountain, and Kincaid Cochrane was pressed against her. She giggled as he kissed her neck and nibbled her ear. He stepped back and raised his hand to his mouth.

"Look at that. I got your earring," he mumbled, taking the golden hoop from his clenched teeth and inserting it back into her left pierced lobe.

Ryan felt sick. He backed away from them, but his movement caught their attention. Bea's eyes widened and her jaw dropped. Kincaid looked sheepish but said nothing. Ryan continued to back up until he made it around the corner.

Stunned, he tried to gather his wits. The show was about to start, and only one thing was clear: he needed to find a different route to the auditorium.

13

Ramona Johns stared down at her brother's fertility clinic, willing the lights to come back on, willing the limousine by the curb to reappear, but she had missed the final act of the meeting. Dropping her finished cigarette in the ashtray, she left the porch and went into the second-story condo with the purpose of changing into her standard garb of elastic-waist black pants, a floral smock top, and clogs. It was warm enough not to need a jacket. She peeked in on her mother, asleep in her double bed, and resisted the impulse to cover her bare legs with the blanket she'd kicked aside. She shut the door, left the condo, and headed downstairs to the parking lot, running a comb through her waist-length dark hair as she walked.

Her Impala was a mobile garbage dump, with food wrappers, plastic bags, and cups littering the front and back seats. She cleared an uneaten brown-bagged lunch that contained an old peanut butter sandwich and a spotted, rotting banana off the driver's seat before she lowered herself into the car and settled into the seat as though it were a nest. She knew where to find her brother.

Cruising down the strip, she turned down a small street near the Hacienda Hotel and pulled into the parking lot of the Dippy

Dive. Labelle's *Lady Marmalade* blasted out through the open front door, held in place with concrete blocks. No need for a bouncer at this bar. It was classic seventies basement game room chic, with a glittery laminated bar, red stools, and a checkered floor. The unadorned, dimly lit back room was where Ramona would find the good doctor.

Mawmaw had taken a fifteen-year break from childbearing between Wendall and Ramona, who had turned nineteen on August first. With such an age gap between Wendall and his baby sister, Wendall often thought of himself as her caretaker, and in all actuality, he had been. MawMaw had him change her diapers and watch her at a time when Wendall would have preferred hanging out with his friends, skateboarding back alleys, and sneaking into the pool area at Caesars, where they could watch girls sunbathe. There were times when Wendall resented his little charge, but there were other times when he saw how much joy Ramona brought their ailing mother. It was at these times he knew Ramona was a blessing, and it directly influenced Wendall's decision to go into the field of fertility when he finished medical school.

The jukebox was playing Bachman-Turner Overdrive's *You Ain't Seen Nothin' Yet* when Ramona stepped into the back room, where the poker game was in progress. Wendall sat with three of his friends, all of whom Ramona recognized.

Chris looked up when he saw her. "Hey, Ramona, join us."

Wendall looked up and his face fell. She was the last person he wanted to see at the Dive.

Years shy of becoming the doctor who would someday meet Zella, Wendall's thick head of hair was untouched by gray, and his long face was unlined. He did not yet need glasses to see the cards in his hand.

Ramona leaned over her big brother and breathed on him, causing him to shift uncomfortably in his chair.

Travis gave a cursory glance at Ramona's ample derrierre and couldn't hide his smile. "What brings you by?"

Ramona ignored Travis. She didn't like his acne and was horrified by his interest in her. She poked her finger at her brother's cards. "That's good, right? What are you playing?"

"No-limit hold 'em," Bill told her.

Wendall glared up at her. "Why don't you tell everyone what I've got?"

"I will, if you confirm that Elvis was at the clinic tonight."

Chris whistled low and guffawed. "Elvis at the sperm bank. Right."

Wendall shot him a look, then put his hand facedown on the table. "I think you need to stop drinking, Ramona."

"I haven't been drinking."

"Then stop smoking."

"Stop smoking what?" Both hands were on her hips now.

The men laughed.

Wendall picked his cards back up, and pushed seven twenties toward the center of the table. "I'll open the pot for a hundred-forty."

"I call," Chris said.

On the button, Travis looked down at his hand. He made the call, and then Bill raised it to six hundred and ninety. Wendall folded, Chris made the call, and Travis decided to move. He grabbed a handful of chips and a stack of cash and re-raised three hundred. Bill moved all-in.

Wendall got up and steered his sister toward the door. "Do you know how late it is?"

Ramona was defiant. "Of course."

"And you left MawMaw home alone?"

"She's sleeping. She's fine. Tell me about Elvis."

A wry smile formed on Wendall's lips. "He's the King of Rock and Roll."

"And he was at your clinic tonight."

Wendall was firm. "No. Stop imagining things and go home."

"Fine," Ramona pouted. "Lie about it. But I know what I saw."

"You shut up about my clinic and stay away from my card games."

Ramona pushed him aside and looked at the guys. "He had a ten of spades, a jack of diamonds, two ducks, and a five of clubs."

A cheer went up from the table. They hadn't even heard her.

Bill's cards were down—he had a ten to ace straight, all spades. He raked the pile of twenties toward him, ready to count to his fortune.

Ramona gave her brother one last dirty look, turned on her heel, and marched out of the room. Silent for a moment, Wendall watched her go. Then he looked back at the table, where a new hand was being dealt.

14

Ryan stood in the wings offstage and wanted to throw up, not because he was nervous to perform but because he'd seen Kincaid kiss Bea. He buried his face in the folds of the heavy velvet curtains and was sure his knees were about to buckle. The show's emcee, Steve, an eighth grader ready to make the leap to Pace High School for the Performing Arts in the coming year, warmed up the audience with a few off-colored jokes which were booed. Then he welcomed Ryan to the stage, prefacing his entrance with warm words.

"Not since Leith Black performed on our stage ten years ago has our school witnessed talent to match his. That was then. This is now. You may already know him. He may sit next to you in biology or choir or math. His name is Ryan Wyatt, and he not only sings, he writes songs too. I haven't found out yet whether or not he can dance."

The audience laughed as a courtesy. Humor was not Steve's forte. Ryan peeked out of a break in the curtains to scan the audience. His parents were in the third row. His mom had the video camera up and running, and his dad was staring at something in his lap. Bea was nowhere in sight.

"So, without further ado, here's Ryan Wyatt."

Ryan dropped the curtain, picked up his guitar, shook his legs one at a time, and walked to the center of the stage, where the microphone was placed. Steve disappeared stage left. Ryan was alone. He stepped up to the mic and cleared his throat.

"Hopefully, you all left the tacos in the dining hall so there's nothing to throw."

A wave of laughter echoed back at him.

"I'm going to sing a song for you tonight that honors all the great singers and how they had their time to shine. Some of them are still with us, and others, not so much. But in their time, they made music, they made memories, and they touched us with their art."

Ryan sang the verse from Aretha to Little Richard, and the audience spontaneously began to clap along right as he launched into the chorus. They were a half-beat behind, but he slowed his guitar playing to match them, and collectively, the rhythmic thunderclaps filled the auditorium and carried the song forward. They quieted for the verse that took them from Orbison to Morrison, and then erupted into rhythmic claps for the chorus again. Finishing it off with a repeat of the chorus, Ryan took a bow and looked out at the sea of smiling faces. Applause swelled like a tidal wave, threatening to crash the stage and wash him away. Someone called out for more. Then he saw Bea in silhouette, lit from the hallway behind, as she peered into the auditorium from the entrance in back, below the balcony. He stared down at his mother, the red light on her video recorder a steady beacon, her smile irrepressible. Beside her, his dad looked non-plussed, unimpressed, perhaps even a bit restless and eager for the show to be over.

"I'd like to sing something special I wrote for a friend not long ago in commemoration of the holiday season. I know some of you are Christian. I know some of you are Jewish. I think we might even have a Buddhist or two out there. And we definitely have some atheists." Laughter swept toward him and the realization he was accepted filled him with warmth. "But whatever you are or aren't, I think the holiday season is a time of celebration, regardless of one's faith. It's a time to appreciate those you love and connect with, and a time to believe in miracles. I hope you enjoy it."

The audience settled back into their seats, expectant.

When we walked the other day, There was so much I could say, But I didn't say a thing, Because my heart had taken wing, You're my Christmas miracle, Right here by my side, You're my Christmas miracle, It can't be denied, Simple are the things we share, Bus rides, bike rides, here to there, Talking, texting, all day long, While I try to write this song, You're my Christmas miracle, All wrapped up with a bow, But I will love you all year long, Just thought that you should know... Just thought that you should know.

The simple tune was the perfect complement to his first, weightier number, and the audience was on his feet.

He wanted to relish the standing ovation, but he could not. After he finished *Christmas Miracle*, he watched as Kincaid joined Bea at the auditorium door and then led her away, allowing the door to swing shut behind them.

15

Logan was lying atop a pile of dirty clothes, reading a Batman comic book while his parents fought in the other room about how Jarrod must have thrown out something Ramona wanted saved, when someone knocked loudly on the Lockharts' front door.

"It's the police," Logan muttered under his breath, unaware of his prescience. He tried to roll over but the pile of socks, underwear, and jeans was too uneven. He got up, snapped on a light, and flopped down on his stomach again.

The arguing stopped. His father or mother must have answered the door.

Then he heard his mother shriek. "What?"

Curious, Logan threw down the comic book and wandered out into the hallway. He peered around the corner.

Two officers from the Santa Monica Code Enforcement Division stood outside, staring at Logan's parents through the latched screen door.

"I'm sorry we were loud," Ramona said, worried that a neighbor had complained.

The officer who spoke wore a nametag that read "Dwight Napier."

"That's not why we're here. We're here about the mess in your yard."

Ramona was offended. "Mess?"

"Yes, ma'am," the second officer, Paul Wedder, said. "We enforce code violations, and your yard needs to be cleaned up."

Jarrod came to the door.

"They say our yard is a mess," Ramona whined.

"Well, it is."

"And we need to clean it up."

"I've been telling you that for years."

"What's wrong with the yard?" Ramona demanded.

"We can show you if you'd like," Napier said.

Jarrod unlatched the screen door. "Come through the house."

The men came inside and picked their way through the debris in the living room, through the wall-to-wall garbage in the kitchen, to the door. As they tromped through, Wedder nudged Napier. Both were visibly alarmed at the hoarding, and Wedder stopped to make a note on the pad he carried. "So, you guys have a lot of kids?" he asked.

"Just the one," Jarrod said.

Logan waited till they were outside before he stumbled to the kitchen, clearing a space on the counter beneath the window so he could watch.

His mom's face was red as Napier pointed to the thirty-two gallon tubs stuffed with items Ramona had picked up from thrift stores. Some of the merchandise was in garbage bags, and a teddy bear arm was sticking out of the top of a canvas sack, making it look as though the loveworn toy was waving for help. Jarrod had a pile of car parts and tools stacked near the garage, where a motorcycle was in a state of reassembly. Palm branches that had fallen during windstorms lay scattered across the backyard like dried octopus tentacles. Even newspapers and magazines, stacked and bundled, stood near the fence by the outdoor grill that had tipped over and spilled used charcoal.

Officer Wedder ripped a ticket off his pad and handed it to Jarrod.

As Jarrod and Ramona walked back to the house with the officers, Logan started to get off the counter, but he slipped and landed on the floor. Pots and pans that had been stacked precariously by the sink crashed down. He sat up quickly, hoping he still had time to escape, but, hearing the clatter, the adults stepped up their pace and were back in the kitchen before Logan had time to get away.

"Is that your son?" Napier asked.

Jarrod grunted and slipped through a narrow space to help him up.

"When's the last time you were able to cook anything in here?" Wedder wanted to know.

Ramona stared blankly at the stove, which was piled with boxes and dirty dishes. *How dare he?* She cooked whenever she felt motivated to clear the mess away, but the mounds of trash always crept back.

Jarrod examined his son. "Are you okay?"

Embarrassed, Logan nodded and ran out of the room.

16

After the show, Ryan and Bea's parents stood in the hallway, waiting to congratulate him. Bea's father, Jay Edwin, was a successful talent agent who represented Keisha Theron, Julia Burstyn, and Diane Annisten in film, the kid who liked Poofy Pops in the cereal commercial everyone parroted, and Victoria's Secret model Hilary Winslet. He was also a consummate collector of art and eclectic items from the past hundred years, and he often attended public auctions to win treasures. Bea's mom Heather Edwin ran a dance studio in the San Fernando Valley, co-owned by a gal pal who taught strippers how to work the pole every night from midnight until six in the morning.

Ryan liked both of them and they, in turn, treated him like the son they never had. He only wished his own dad was as enthusiastic about supporting him emotionally.

Jay ruffled Ryan's hair. "Great job, kiddo."

Heather grabbed his arm. "You're ruining his Elvis 'do!"

Tonight, dressed in a dark wool suit brightened by a scarlet ascot, Jay resembled a young Ted Knight from *The Mary Tyler Moore Show*. "You think this kid looks like Elvis?"

"Yes, he looks like Elvis." Heather wore a rose-colored silk blouse, burgundy slacks, and low-heeled shoes. The coat tucked under her arm was white faux fur, and it looked like she was holding a fluffy rabbit. Her right eye was lazy, so it was hard for Ryan to look directly at her whenever they had a conversation.

Zella was beaming. "I recorded the whole show."

"Thanks, Mom." Ryan waited for his dad to say something. He doubted Gene even knew Zella had been teaching him magic tricks after school, using props she'd acquired in Vegas when she dreamt of doing her own show.

Jay spoke up. "Where's Bea?"

Heather looked around. "Yeah, where is she?"

Jay rested his hand on Ryan's shoulder. "Dinner this Thursday?"

Ryan had been eating dinner with Bea and her parents every Thursday night for the past three years. "I don't know. I think Bea may be busy."

Jay was just about to argue the point that Ryan was welcome in their home regardless of his daughter's plans when a large woman in a poncho approached, grabbed Ryan, and kissed him on both cheeks. Baffled, he looked around.

"Darling," she exclaimed. "Your performance was magnificent! Riveting."

Ryan cleared his throat. "Thank you."

The woman beamed at the Wyatts and Edwins. "Which of you are his parents?"

Zella spoke up. "We are."

The woman's eyes darted back and forth between Zella and Gene. "Do either of you sing?"

"I'm tone deaf," Gene told her.

"I sing in the shower, but my voice isn't very strong," Zella admitted.

"My son is Steve Seton," the large woman explained. "I'm Cynthia, his mom. Neither of you sing? You would think there would be a genetic predisposition for it."

Gene shrugged. "Guess not."

"Well, one of your parents must sing then. Or sang."

Zella and Gene looked at each other but said nothing.

"Anyway," Cynthia resumed. "I just wanted to compliment young Ryan on his lovely voice."

"Thank you," Zella replied.

Cynthia grabbed both of Ryan's cheeks in her chubby fingers. "You watch out for this one. He's gonna be something someday." After this pronouncement, she kissed Ryan on the nose and backed up. With a wave of her hand, she swept down the hallway.

Ryan offered his parents and the Edwins a weak smile. "Excuse me."

He slunk off in the opposite direction Mrs. Seton had gone, dragging his guitar case. The hallway linoleum had been recently buffed, and the black and white speckles of confetti embedded in the beige squares sparkled beneath the ceiling lights.

"Probably going to wash that bright red lipstick off his face," Jay joked.

"He did sound good," Heather said. "I never heard that first song before, the one about the rock and roll legends. I wonder who wrote it?"

"I think he did," Zella said. Tonight, she wore a red pashmina over slacks and a gray sweater, and her dark hair was pinned up. The tiny semi-precious red stones that sparkled in her earlobes matched the stones in the bracelet on her left wrist.

"He didn't write that," Gene said. "He couldn't have."

"Why couldn't he have?"

"He's in junior high, Zella."

"I'm pretty sure I heard him working on it after school," Zella disagreed.

"I'm sure you heard him working on it, but that doesn't mean he wrote it."

Zella started to pick at the edge of her pashmina.

Heather attempted to restore the peace. "Whatever, it was lovely. And the Christmas one was too."

17

The woman from Child Protective Services appeared on the Lockharts' doorstep three days after officers from the Santa Monica Code Enforcement Division paid a visit. After knocking on the screen door and ringing the bell without a response, she sat down on the stoop and pulled Stephen King's *Misery* out of her oversized handbag so she could read while she waited. Jarrod's beloved black Chevelle SS 396 was parked in the driveway, and behind that sat Ramona's ride—a royal blue Oldsmobile Vista Cruiser packed front to back with plastic bags stuffed with clothing, bric-a-brac, and yard-sale pickings. Both parents were home. The woman from CPS was being ignored.

The hinges on the front door creaked as she turned the page. A young boy stood behind the latched screen door, and the foul mixture of stale cigarettes, urine, and rotting food assaulted her so forcibly, she jerked her head back. Though it was a warm Saturday afternoon, the boy wore ripped thermal underwear and a tank undershirt that didn't hide his emaciated torso and the bruises on his arms. His chestnut-colored hair was unwashed. Greasy hanks covered his ears and fell into his dark eyes, set deep in orbits discolored from trauma and lack of sleep.

The woman stood up, smoothed down the legs of her brown jersey slacks, and smiled. "You must be Logan."

Solemn, Logan nodded.

"Are you parents home?"

Logan tried to figure out what the pretty lady wanted. Her hair was the color of honey, held back from her face with two tortoiseshell combs, and she smelled like vanilla cake. She didn't have anything with her other than her purse and the thick book she was reading, so she wasn't selling anything. And she wasn't wearing a uniform, so she wasn't law enforcement. Maybe she was from his school. He had been sick a lot lately and had missed some important lessons.

"They're out back," Logan said, "in the yard."

"Behind the house?"

Logan nodded.

"Do you have a dog?"

Logan frowned, stared at his bare feet, and shook his head.

Peering through the screen, Angela Campbell noticed open-topped boxes and Rubbermaid containers stuffed with everything from clothing to vases to lamps.

"Are you moving?"

"No. It's always like this. My mom likes flea markets."

"I can see that. Can I come in?"

Logan's eyes widened, and he took a step back. The screen was latched, so he knew she couldn't get in, but he was alarmed.

"It's okay," she soothed. "I'll just go around back and talk to your parents."

Logan watched her head down the steps toward the driveway. When she was far enough away, he unlatched the screen and stepped out onto the stoop just in time to see her disappear around the side of the garage where the gate to the backyard was. At a safe distance, he began to follow her.

The lady needed to shout to be heard over the argument Ramona and Jarrod were having over whether or not to throw out an old hard-plastic wading pool with a cracked bottom. Nearly five feet in circumference, Ramona held it in front of her like a body shield while she argued. It came up to her nose, leaving only her wild eyes and mussed long dark hair in view. Jarrod was trying to tug it away from her, but she held onto it with ferocity she only displayed when it came to her possessions and the possibility of parting with them.

"It's cracked! It's unusable! It's for babies! Logan isn't a baby anymore!"

"You can seal the crack with tape," Ramona argued. "It'll be fine."

"Mr. and Mrs. Lockhart!" The gate swung open and the woman entered the bleak yard, nearly tripping over a hand-push mower propped against the garage. As the gate was swinging shut, Logan caught it and followed the woman.

Ramona looked overheated. "Who are you?"

The woman approached, extending a business card as she did so.

Ramona loosened her grip on the cracked pool to accept it and Jarrod, ashamed of the tug-of-war with his wife, stepped a few respectful feet back.

Ramona was filled with contempt. "Child Protective Services!"

"Yes, ma'am. I believe Officers Napier and Wedder came out this week to tell you that you need to clean up your yard?" Angela looked around at the debris and stacks of rotting wood, bricks, containers, and trash bags stuffed with someone else's unwanted belongings. A broken preschool xylophone pierced the side of one bag, its keyboard rusted and discolored. The thirty-two gallon tubs overflowing with items from thrift stores, the garbage bags stuffed with merchandise, the haphazardly-stacked pile of car parts and tools, the fallen palm branches, the tipped grill that spewed charcoal, and the bundled newspapers and magazines near the fence—all noted by the officers—hadn't been moved or discarded. "Are you making any progress?"

"Does it look like it?" Jarrod asked.

Angela smiled at him. His frustration was palpable. His nails were chewed and dirty, his plaid shirt was ripped in front, and sweat dripped from his furrowed brow.

Ramona wasn't about to calm down. "I thought this was about code violations."

"That's part of it."

"Tell her what can happen if we don't get the yard up to code," Jarrod prompted.

"I believe that you'll need to pay a fine, and then, after that, if the yard is still not brought up to code, you'll go to court. With sufficient evidence, your home can and will be taken from you if you can't or won't comply with the law."

"How is that?" Ramona raged. "We pay our mortgage every month!"

"That's not the point," Jarrod told her.

Angela remained calm. "I'm here about your son."

Pressed up against the side of the garage, Logan listened closely.

"The officers seem to think the inside of your home might present..." She paused to choose her words carefully and ascertain she had Ramona's full attention. "The inside of your home may not be a safe environment for your son. You're going to need to clean up inside too, so we can inspect the living conditions and make sure there aren't any rotting floorboards, exposed wires, mold, and the like. If conditions are unsafe and remain so, Logan can and will be taken from you."

Ramona was apoplectic. "This is Wendall's fault, isn't it?"

"I'm sorry, ma'am. Wendall?"

"My brother! My brother called you!"

"No, ma'am. I assure you, my coming here today was based solely on reports the officers filed."

Ramona spat on the ground at Angela's feet. "I don't believe you."

The woman reached deep inside her purse and extracted a slip of paper, which she handed to Jarrod. "I'll stop by in the next week or two, unannounced, to check in on you."

Ramona tried to swing the unwieldy pool at Angela and nearly fell down. Her face was red with rage. "You do that! You just try and come back and take my son!"

Then she collapsed and began to sob, one hand still clutching the pool.

18

Zella wore a pink flannel shirt with the sleeves ripped off and a nondescript faded mauve baseball cap for her afternoon of work in the backyard garden. She was planting miniature hollyhocks when Ryan skateboarded through the back gate and down the concrete path next to the pool. Nana was paddling about in the water to cool off from the heat, but when she saw Ryan, she clambered out of the shallow end, shook her fur vigorously, and ran to him.

"Hey, girl." He fell onto the grass beside the path and she jumped on top of him, giving her coat another shake, soaking him.

"There's a towel on the lounge," Zella shouted, giving a wave.

Before she called to him, Ryan hadn't noticed his mother. Taking his skateboard with him, he got up, got the towel, gave Nana a thorough rubdown, and went to sit beside Zella. "This is a great time," he told her. His nearly-year-round tan hadn't faded during the recent bout of rain that lasted more than ten days, and he was looking healthy, if a bit somber. Year round, they spent hours in the yard, swimming, barbecuing, and gardening. A bit of chill meant nothing as long as the sun was bright.

Zella raised the brim of her cap. "A great time for what?"

Ryan reached for the vintage Alva skateboard Mr. Edwin had given him after winning it in a storage auction. It was flipped over so the wheels and the angular "Alva" in black script on wood the color of honey showed. "See these wheels?" He spun the back two. "They're kryptonics. That's what the old-school skateboarders rode on concrete in skate parks and swimming pools because they're the hardest ones made. I was thinking of doing some aerials in the pool. You think we can empty it?"

Zella reached for the skateboard and flipped it upright so the angularly scripted Alva logo, in red and gold on black, was visible. She ran her fingers over the sparkly grip tape. "Are you serious?"

"Totally." He lay down in the grass and stared at the clouds. One had a perfect hole in the center as though a cannonball had been shot through its center.

"You'll probably have to damage the drain at the bottom so we have a plausible excuse to empty it. Otherwise, your dad would never go for it."

Ryan couldn't believe his mother was humoring him. "You're kidding."

Zella shrugged. "Maybe. So how are you doing with the magic rings?" She had given him a set from her days in Vegas, and he had been practicing the illusion of joining and separating them in front of his bedroom mirror.

"Fine. Still working with them."

"Do you want to help me with some of these?" Zella indicated more than a dozen potted pink hollyhocks she wanted planted in front of her lilac shrubs.

"Only if you tell me more secrets from the days you were an understudy for that magician's assistant. You know, before Dad took you away from all that and you had me."

"Ah, yes, career thwarted." Nana came over, settled herself, and put her head on Zella's bare knee. "You want to know more magic. Where do I begin?"

19

"Wendall, is that you?" Ramona stomped around the living room, knocking over boxes and containers like a rampaging animal.

It was four in the afternoon. Logan's dad was at work and his mom was yelling at his Uncle Wendall on her cell phone. A fleeting impulse to dash from his room and jump on her back to get her to stop rippled through him. Instead, he sat down in the doorway to his room and leaned against a container full of yard-sale clothes that were too large for him.

"You did this!" Ramona raged. "You never liked me being a mom and you're going to have Logan taken away! What am I talking about? You should know! You're the one who sent CPS here! Well, City Code Enforcement is crawling all over us for violating their precious regulations, aren't they?" She paused and took a gulping breath of air before she continued. "No, that part's not about Logan, it's about the house. We've got to get the house up to code or—well, they gave us a warning, but I had a little trouble getting rid of some stuff. Everything means something to me! Jarrod tries to throw it away, and I tell him, easy for you, it don't mean nothing to you, it's easy for you to throw it away, but it means something to me. There's a court date set on the seventeenth. They slapped us with a fine and now they're going to put a lien on the house! They're going to condemn it! Where are we supposed to live? And CPS is up my ass like a blind man in the woods! Something about the floorboards going, the ceiling caving in, exposed wires. Said the place stinks, like they can't even breathe in here. Well, I'm breathing fine and I don't smell anything. They want me to admit I'm doing something wrong and endangering Logan! Do they care about me? No! They care about Logan. Well, that's the big tip-off, isn't it? Once they got involved,

I knew it had something to do with you! You always wanted a son, didn't you? Well, you can't have Logan, got it? You're trying to get me to lose MawMaw's home *and* my son! I've hated you my whole life, and I despise you even *more* now! And for your information, that night at your clinic, I did see Elvis, and I'll take that truth to my grave!"

Ramona disconnected the call and threw her cell phone across the room. When it hit the edge of MawMaw's portrait, it cracked, slid down the wall, and ended up behind a stack of board games snapped up at a rummage sale. Ramona collapsed into a heap in a compact space between two thick cubes—one containing candlesticks and broken lamps, and the other, moth-riddled blankets—and began to cry.

Logan picked his way down the hall and into the living room, wading through debris to reach her. After school that day, he'd put on dirty Spider-Man pajamas, which he'd outgrown but still loved. His brown eyes widened at the sight of his mother reduced to a wailing mass on the threadbare carpet.

She stopped long enough to notice Logan's bare feet. Then her eyes traveled up to his smudge-marked face. "Hi, honey. Go get my cigarettes for me, will ya?"

"Where are they?"

Ramona wore a blank expression as she mentally retraced her steps back from the living room, into the kitchen. "The kitchen stove. On top of the stack, in a cake pan."

Logan made his way along a path cleared wide enough to accommodate his obese mother and entered the kitchen. Then he stood on a chair, felt around in the topmost pan, retrieved the cigarettes, ashtray, and Zippo, got down, and returned to his mother. With a shaky hand, Ramona knocked a cigarette out of the pack, lit it, and took a deep drag.

"Who was on the phone?"

"Your Uncle Wendall. You don't remember him. He came to see MawMaw before she met her eternal reward."

Ramona always used that expression when she talked about death. Even when Logan's hamster died—lost and forgotten and crushed by a tipped dresser, she had told him Hambidextrous, nicknamed Dex, had gone on to his eternal reward, which Logan pictured as a shiny wheel to run laps on, endless Evian on tap to quench his thirst, wood shavings from a million pencils for bedding, and a boatload of sunflower seeds, walnuts, and sliced apples anytime he needed a nibble.

But Ramona was wrong about Logan not remembering his Uncle Wendall, who, when MawMaw was on her deathbed, took him aside and taught him a song that went, "This old man, he played one, He played knick-knack on my thumb; With a knick-knack paddy-whack, Give a dog a bone, This old man came rolling home." After memorizing the song all the way to ten and singing it together, they went outside and threw a big plastic ball Uncle Wendall had brought with him in his big white Cadillac.

It was easy to remember a man who was kind enough to spend time with him, a man with a warm smile and an easygoing manner who smelled of tropical cologne instead of stale cigarettes and beer. When Wendall gave him a hug, Logan whispered, "Uncle Coconuts" in his ear, and the man was delighted. He laughed heartily, which empowered Logan to grab him again so he could share his secret.

"You should stay here," he whispered. "This place is Crazy Town."

Logan's uncle raised an eyebrow. "That bad, eh?"

Logan threw his arms around him and clung to him, not wanting to let him go. Ramona saw this through the front screen door, started to holler, and Logan and Wendall broke apart, startled.

But Logan's dysfunctional family life at the time of MawMaw's passing paled in comparison to how bad things finally got. It was a time of transition from bad to worse, before Ramona began buying everything she wanted from flea markets, online auctions, and swap meets, before the house started filling up with garbage, before Ramona's smoking increased from a pack a day to three, before she buried the stovetop with old pots and pans and stopped cooking regularly, and before Jarrod found reasons not to be home while his wife smothered her broken emotions with things, things, and more things that piled up, sagged the floorboards, made their home a dump, and threatened to eclipse them all.

20

The lyrics floated from Ryan's room, from beneath the locked door, through the gap between the wood and frame not wide enough to slip a letter through, and they pierced Zella's heart. *Putting pictures on the wall, can't believe they never fall. Don't believe I know them all. Who was I way back when? Sick and wrapped in torn sheets as the streets were flowing red, mangled, shredding at their feet, haloes glowing round their heads, I was lying in defeat, badly broken, nearly dead. Can you help me? Can you help? That was all I said.*

Zella shuddered, took a deep breath, and knocked. The music stopped. Inside his room, still decorated like Ariel the mermaid's fantasy pad, Ryan fell silent. Zella tried the door handle.

"Just a minute, Mom."

She heard the bedsprings creak as Ryan got up. He opened the door a crack and peered out at her. "What's up?"

Ryan was now sixteen, a junior in high school, dealing with an emotional absent father and friends who were into drugs.

"Can I come in?"

He opened the door wide enough for her to pass through. She took a seat at his desk and turned to face him as he flopped down on his bed and nudged his guitar with his foot so it was out of the way. He grew more handsome as each year passed, his dark hair thick and wavy, his skin unblemished, his eyes the clearest blue, his nose as classic as that of Michelangelo's David, his jaw strong, his bottom lip so full it looked Botoxed.

"I heard you're going out with your father to see a house after school tomorrow to see how he works, what he does."

"Yeah. We've been arguing. I'm going to see if we can reach common ground."

"That's very mature of you. Sounds like something a parent would say. Have you been talking to Mr. Edwin?"

Ryan closed his eyes. He hadn't had a good, long talk with the Edwins since the night Bea kissed Kincaid. It was as if the closeness they once shared was as insignificant now as the dust motes floating between the open slats on his shuttered bedroom windows. Neither had he been over to their house, despite its proximity to his own, though he did see the Edwins in their yard from time to time, and his mother was right—it was Mr. Edwin who told him to make an effort with his dad before things became irreparable. Mrs. Edwin still asked him to dinner whenever she spotted him outside, but Ryan always declined. Instead, he spent his free time with three buddies who liked to get high, listen to music, and use fake IDs so they could get into nightclubs on weekends.

"Was that a new song you wrote?"

Despite the fact he was lying down, Ryan managed to shrug. "I'm not so sure about writing songs anymore. I haven't been inspired for a long time now."

"But you're a natural performer," Zella protested. "Just like me."

Ryan sat up. "You had fun, huh?"

"Did you know I still have a trunkful of magic stuff I never showed you? It's in the rafters over the workbench. Come on, come outside with me and help me pull it down."

Curious, Ryan got up and followed his mom out of his room, down the stairs, and out to the garage. Using a ladder, he brought down the dusty silver trunk she specified, and together, they dragged it into backyard, past Nana, fast asleep by the pool, next to her water bowl. Facing each other, they took lawn chairs at opposite ends of the latched trunk, and Ryan took a deep breath. Then Zella unfastened the lid, threw it back, and they both peered inside.

21

Things were going downhill fast at the Lockhart home. In full avoidance mode, Jarrod spent more time away, chroming bumpers and selling drugs, only coming home to see if his wife and son were alive—if miserable—and had a few dollars to spend before he headed out again. Bagging drifts of accumulated goods like fallen leaves and putting them out at the curb had backfired. That week, Ramona hauled a Hefty bag back inside, dumped it out, and began to scream as she held up a plastic container of baby powder.

She shook the container for emphasis, and it rattled. "Do you see this?"

Jarrod's hands were in fists at his hips and his face was haggard. "What?"

She sat on the edge of a set of Rubbermaid drawers and unscrewed the lid to the container, dumping the contents into her pudgy open palm. "Look!"

Costume jewelry and rings with synthetic stones she had bought on QVC filled her hand and spilled over onto a pile magazines stacked on the rug. She looked like a pirate sifting through gold doubloons. "This one I got last year, this one I got when MawMaw died, and this one I got just last month."

She held up a ring embedded with tourmaline chips and Jarrod took it from her.

"What is that, green bottle glass?"

She screamed and snatched it away. "No!"

"Who keeps their jewelry in an old baby powder container?"

"I do! What if someone broke in and robbed us?"

A vein throbbed on Jarrod's forehead. "They'd never find it in this landfill!"

"That's right! Because everything precious is hidden in something unexpected! The first thing burglars would look for is a jewelry box!"

Jarrod willed himself to calm down. Then, as though a switch had been flipped, he shrugged and walked to the door, looking wasted, thin, and as dirty as his son.

"I gotta go."

He cast a rueful look at Logan, who stood there in gray long johns, holding a dogeared issue of Spider-Man. On the cover, against a yellow sky, Spider-Man traversed between buildings, his right foot forward. The comic was ripped in the corner. The superhero was missing his non-web shooting hand that should have been in the upper right-hand corner.

As Jarrod went out the front door, he let the screen door bang.

Ramona dumped her jewelry back into the powder canister.

"Logan, go latch that."

Dutifully, Logan did as told. Then, he had an idea. "Mom, you know how MawMaw's room is the only place in the house that's clean?"

Ramona scoffed. "I don't keep a dirty house."

Logan took her by the hand. "Come with me."

The door to MawMaw's room creaked on its hinges when he pushed it inward. The room smelled of musty flowers and Vicks

VapoRub, which Ramona slathered on her mother's chest, arms, and legs when she complained of everything from congestion to sore muscles. Of course, it never helped the cancer; it was her daughter's ministrations that made MawMaw feel better. Her painkillers were kept in a side table, and a fresh pitcher of ice water was replenished three times a day. Logan could still picture her propped up in bed, with four pillows beneath her head and back, a scarf on her grayed head, bundled in her robe, even though she was beneath two blankets. The window stood open and a breeze blew the sheer curtains embroidered with sunflowers at the hemline. She didn't read or watch TV. Instead, she played solitaire with an old deck of cards adorned with Chester the Cheetah, the big-faced cat in sunglasses, a promotional item given away at the grocery store at a time when Ramona was going through a family-sized bag of Cheetos every day.

When Logan would visit MawMaw in her room, he'd sit at the end of the bed and she'd have him guess whether the card she was holding was red or black. Once, he got four out of five correct. They had all been black. One time he told her he thought, instead of the Kings, Queens, and Jacks, the artist should have put Chester's face on the royalty, and MawMaw threw her head back into the pillows and laughed till she gasped for air. She was missing teeth in the back of her mouth instead of the front, like many old people with infrequent dental care, and he wondered if she'd swallowed them. After she died, Logan went into her room, took a jar of the mentholated rub from her side table drawer, and looked in her dresser. Weeks after the funeral, all of her belongings were still neatly folded in the drawers, the right amount in each one, none on them overfilled. Logan touched the nylons and garter belts, girdles and bras she must have worn years ago. There was even a box of maxi pads that looked like diapers, which didn't embarrass him as much as he thought it might. They were more a curiosity, the big pads with a set of instructions that showed a woman fitting a pad into clips on an elastic belt that made her look like she was wearing the letter "Y" below her waist. The dresses in the closet were all size nine, and many had rhinestone buttons, lacy collars, and large pockets. There was a carton of Camel Lights on the high shelf, shoeboxes with tissue sticking out from under the lids, scrapbooks, and a large stuffed Steiff bear Grandpa had given her after they met. The only things Ramona had taken from the room that belonged to her mother were the Elvis albums and the small tabletop stereo with tinny speakers. They were now in an unused room in the four-bedroom house, a catchall room where Ramona liked to listen to music and reminisce back to when MawMaw was alive and life was good.

Logan sat his mom down on the side of the bed and told her to stay put. Then, he went and got a single Rubbermaid container that wasn't too heavy to drag and brought it into the room.

"Let's pretend, okay?"

Ramona sighed deeply. "Is this going to take long? Go get my cigarettes."

Logan found an unopened pack, a lighter, and an ashtray, and brought them to her. Instead of arguing with him that she already had an open pack and didn't want them to go stale, she unwrapped the cellophane on the fresh pack of cigarettes, tapped one out, and lit it.

Logan took that as a good sign she just might listen.

22

Once Zella unlatched the trunk and threw back the lid, she moved aside so Ryan could look inside. He was dressed in a blue t-shirt and jeans, his image reflected back on the inside mirrored lid as he reached in and brought things out.

Dressed in overall shorts and a form-fitting ribbed white tee, Zella sat on the lawn, her elbows on her raised knees. Her feet were bare, and her lustrous hair was clipped up. Between her youthful demeanor and the fact she was keeping her looks as she aged, she seemed more like her son's older sister than his mother.

Ryan pulled out a clear bag containing a stainless steel sheathed blade, a circular base, and a set of Styrofoam cups. "What's this?"

Zella jumped up with the grace of a young athlete and nearly skipped over to the picnic table near the pool. "Come over here."

A few feet from the table, Nana woke, gave her head a shake, and barked once.

"You can be our audience, girl," Ryan told her. He sat down across from his mother and handed her the bag. Zella removed the blade, unsheathed it, and placed it on the flat wooden table, weatherproofed the previous spring in lacquer the shade of cinnamon. A sudden gust of wind caused the Styrofoam cups to skitter off the table and roll across the lawn. Nana barked again and rose to chase them with Ryan.

He returned with them, winded. "Maybe we should go inside."

"No, this will just take a minute."

He watched as she inserted the blade straight up into a circular base and covered it with one of the cups. Then she placed the other two cups upside down beside it and turned around on the bench. "Okay, mix them up."

Ryan rearranged them and stood up. He examined the cups from different angles to see if he could detect any differences between them and couldn't.

"Okay, you can turn around."

Zella whipped around on the bench, her eyes gleaming. She stood up and studied the cups, then slammed her palm down on the first one, crushing it.

Ryan was horrified. "Mom!"

"It's okay, it's okay." She walked around the table, then back to her side. She crushed the middle cup with her fist next.

"Oh, my God!"

Zella wore a mischievous expression. "What?"

Ryan lifted the third cup off the table. The stainless steel blade glinted in the afternoon sunlight. "How did you know where the knife was?"

Zella lifted up the base and turned it over. Four inches of fishing line had been taped across the bottom so an inch stuck out from beneath the base. The line was so thin it was difficult to see, even when one looked closely.

"You look for that little bit of fishing line."

Ryan was amazed. "I didn't even see it."

"Go get something else."

Feeling enthusiastic, Ryan went over to the trunk and picked out a bag containing a pair of shackles and a key. He returned to the table and started to hand it to her but she waved him off. "You can take them out."

Ryan removed the handcuffs and key and looked at his mom expectantly. She came over to him and put her hands behind her back. "Cuff me."

He hesitated. "Are you sure?"

Held against his mother's delicate wrists, the cuffs looked heavy. Reluctantly, he snapped them on her. They looked like bright bracelets.

"Lock them."

Ryan fit the key in the tiny lock and turned it.

"Test that they're locked."

Ryan tugged. They were secure.

Zella turned around, her back to him. "Okay, sing me a song."

"What?"

"Something happy. I'm tired of your teenage angst."

Ryan broke into a grin and Zella thought he must be the handsomest young man in the world. Their eyes locked, blue on blue. He sang the opening lines to *On The Street Where You Live*, then stopped and looked at her expectantly.

"*My Fair Lady*. Makes me think of you and Bea."

A shadow crossed Ryan's face. Mr. Prescott had them do that musical in fifth grade. Ryan wondered what he was doing now, if he was still teaching. "Harry Connick Jr. did a jazzed up version of that song," he said.

"You don't want to talk about Bea, do you?"

Ryan scowled. "Not much." She had been the only one for him, and her interest in Kincaid had been an abrupt wake-up call.

"Because of how sick she's been?"

"What do you mean?"

Zella was stunned. "You don't know?" She turned her back to him to show she was free of the handcuffs and handed them to him.

The blood had drained from Ryan's face. He needed to sit down.

23

Logan sat in his backyard fort, defeated, and stared through the chain-link fence separating the Lockharts' yard from the Henns' property. The neighboring house was quiet, and it was early evening. He had given up on his mother after trying for hours to get her to sort through her possessions piece by piece, his reasoning being that if she was mad at his dad for discarding boxes without examining the contents, perhaps this careful approach would work better. Everything he showed her, though, was something she wanted to keep: moldy Q-Tips that would never—should never—be used, a candy dish shaped like a basket with a cracked handle, empty L'Eggs pantyhose containers, chipped mugs, dried tubes of paint, stained dishtowels, rag dolls with no arms, an incomplete set of dominoes. It all had to be saved because it meant something to her.

Halfway through the second bin, there was still nothing in the wastebasket he'd brought in from the bathroom, nothing Ramona would dream of throwing away among the dozens of worthless objects Logan had shown her, and she had made a serious dent in the pack of cigarettes he'd brought her. Now she wanted the bottle of gin she kept in the hall closet under a pile of towels, hidden from Jarrod so she could drink it all herself.

Logan went and got a glass and opened the freezer, removing expired frozen foods to find the sole ice tray so he could put some cubes in her drink.

Smoking and drinking on MawMaw's bed, propped against the pillows and feigning fatigue, Ramona continued to shake her head every time her son pulled something else out and held it up. "No, I need to keep that. I might need it someday."

Logan looked at the broken blender, incredulous, and returned it to the box.

And so it went, until half the bottle of gin was gone. He dug around in the box for the next item and when he held it up, he saw that his mother had passed out, her drink spilled on MawMaw's chenille spread, her cigarette still smoldering in the ashtray. Her mouth was open and her head was back, making her look like she was in the middle of a silent scream. Logan kicked the box, took the wastebasket back to the bathroom, and went out back, navigating the cluttered yard until he found a clear spot measuring roughly five feet square. In the failing light, he watched as the stars blinked on like tiny lights. He'd brought some blankets and a pillow outside with him and set about forging a makeshift fort, using surrounding containers as walls. He had no wish to be anywhere near his mother after all he had tried to do, without any appreciation on her part.

He put his head down and dozed. He dreamt he was in a smoky pit and his classmates were throwing hot coals at him. It was hard to breathe, and he coughed. Logan awoke with a start and shook off the nightmare. He peered out of his fort and was stunned. His home—his cluttered, awful home—was on fire, and his mother was inside.

24

Ryan refused to go with his father to show properties unless Nana could come along so, after an argument, they packed the dog into the back of Gene's highly-polished blood red E-Class Cabriolet convertible, fastened a seat belt and looped leashes around her torso to keep her in the car, and headed northwest on North Rexford Drive toward Santa Monica Boulevard.

From there, they were on 405-South for just under a mile, and then they took the I-10 East exit and merged onto the I-10 West to the Pacific Coast Highway. As they hit the coastline, off-shore winds kicked up so Gene and Ryan couldn't converse, but Nana punctuated the road trip with happy barks, her ears flying straight back, her tongue lolling to one side. The ocean rippled, rose, and pounded the shoreline under a Tiffany blue sky, and the beaches were filled with sunbathers.

They were meeting Michael Knight-Lewis, who planned to move to Branson for his own one-man show. Since he grew up in Malibu, he wanted to establish a second home on the West Coast so he could come back out and visit friends from time to time. He had sold his place in Ojai the previous week, so he was anxious to secure a beachfront getaway, pack his bags, head to Missouri, and be back in a few months to visit, after professional decorators furnished his new pad to his specifications.

As Gene pulled up to the Malibu Main Colony, Michael ducked out from beneath one of the winged-doors of his silver McLaren, slammed it shut, and waved. Ryan had seen cars around Beverly Hills that looked like they were straight from *Back to the Future*, but he thought they looked like a pain to get in and out of.

Gene parked behind Michael's car, and Gene and Ryan got out. As Michael approached them, Ryan reached around to untie Nana. His dad's one rule was to keep Nana away from him while was dressed in one of his better suits—a charcoal gray cashmere off-the-rack Brioni, with a purple silk tie and a matching pocket square. Neither Ryan nor Michael had any desire to dress in anything better than jeans and never-iron Dockers for the meet-up, but that didn't bother Gene. Gene dressed to the nines because when he wore a great suit, he felt like he could conquer the world.

Michael gave Nana a scratch on the head. "Big dog."

"150 pounds," Ryan told him.

Gene made the introductions. If Michael thought it odd his agent brought his son and dog along to show him properties, he made no mention of it. The two men talked as Ryan and Nana trailed behind.

Malibu Main was a gated community, and Gene was eager to show Michael a beachfront home with five bedrooms and three-point-five baths worth eight million. The home had an open floorplan that gave the place the expansiveness of an airport hangar. While Gene waxed poetic about the exquisiteness of the French limestone fireplace, Ryan went out onto the patio overlooking the beach. He leaned over one of the solid panes of glass to look at the poles that supported the balcony. Water swirled as waves swept in, and Ryan felt like he was on the bow of a ship.

"You can fish right off the deck," Gene boasted, as the men and Nana joined him.

Michael was glum. "I like the place, I really do, but—"

Gene moved over to the stairs that led down from the balcony to the beach and unlatched the gate. "Look, direct access."

Nana saw the exit and couldn't resist. She ran across the tiled patio and flew down the staircase.

"Nana, no!" Ryan shouted.

Michael was all smiles. "I know about Newfies. They love the water."

"Go and get her, Ryan," Gene commanded.

The men moved to the edge of the balcony to watch Ryan cajole Nana back to shore. Out about thirty yards in no time, Nana barked as she paddled against the waves.

Michael grew serious. "I like the house, I really do, but two of the bedrooms don't face the ocean."

"But two of them do," Gene countered.

Michael shook his head. "Let's keep looking."

25

Logan stood outside in his dirty gray long johns and watched his home, engulfed in flames save for the corner room, where Ramona listened to records on her portable record player. He ran over and tried to peer inside by jumping up and down. After a minute, he gave up. His eyes darted around the yard. A storage box with a firm lid, marked "pillows" in Ramona's spidery scrawl, was three yards away. He dragged it over to the window, climbed on top and looked. The window was open, the screen intact. He pushed on the screen and it sprang forward, into the room now filled with smoke.

He climbed through the open window and landed on the floor with a hard thud. Flames licked at the open doorway. Eyes wild, he searched the room till he located his mother's albums, stacked on a chair near the record player table. The cover of *Elvis' Christmas Album* reflected the light from the flames from the doorway. He grabbed it just as the flames crept closer and began to consume the rug beneath his feet. Scampering to the window, he clambered up, fell through, hit the box of pillows, and rolled onto the grass. Then he ran as fast as he could, out through the side gate, out to the front of his house, out to the street. Lamps and lights were popping on across the street, first in one house, then in a second and a third. Someone would call 911.

Then he saw his dad, three blocks away, in his vintage black Chevelle SS 396, driving like a bat out of hell, barely braking at stop signs. Surely his dad knew the house was on fire and was coming home to save them.

Just as Jarrod entered the block, a mustard-colored sedan careened around the corner and rammed Jarrod's car into the curb. A second car, this one a grimy white, nearly mowed Logan down as it rushed past from the opposite end of the block and rammed the Chevelle's front bumper. Jarrod jumped out as men from both cars sprang from theirs, leaving the doors wide open. One gunshot. Two gunshots. Three. Jarrod fell to the ground, behind his open car door. Logan screamed and the men from the white car turned and noticed him.

"Get the kid," the shorter of the two men shouted, and Logan ran as hard as he could, back to the house, back through the gate into the backyard, and back to the chain-link fence separating his yard from Fred's. He found the gully and shoved the Elvis album beneath the fence before he crawled under it. Then he grabbed the album and hid behind the tree. He heard noise in the yard as the men stumbled over Ramona's bins and boxes. He cringed, held his breath, and waited. In the distance, he heard sirens.

26

It took Ryan a full hour after school to make it to the North Camden florist shop, select a cylindrical vase filled with yellow tulips and goldenrod, return back home, and then head next door to Bea's house, prepared to tell her how sorry he was that he'd ignored her these past years, and why. Of course, she probably knew the reason. After he saw her and Kincaid together in the hallway, he never spoke to her again. He had let the past years slip by, and here he was, sixteen, ready to man up and apologize.

The doorbell sounded like the first six notes to *Anchors Aweigh*, and as Ryan stood on the flagstone porch, he wondered how many times he'd rung it since preschool. Maybe thousands. If she forgave him, he planned to ring the bell daily until they graduated from high school, went off to college, got married, and had kids of their own.

Bea's mom opened the door, and if she was surprised to see him, she covered it well. She was dressed in slacks and a white sweater that looked like it had been sprinkled with multi-colored confetti. Ryan looked directly at her, but it was difficult to tell if she was meeting his gaze because of her wandering eye, which always made her look like she was glancing upward, struggling to remember something important.

"Hi, Mrs. Edwin. Is Bea home?"

"I'm afraid she's resting right now, dear, but come in."

The Edwins had a bench in their entryway which served as a last-chance spot to sit before heading out, a place to wait for someone, something to dump things on if you were just coming home, and somewhere to sit and chat if someone stopped by. Ryan sat on the edge of the corduroy cushion and cradled the flower arrangement in his arms.

"Where are my manners? Here, let me take those."

Mrs. Edwin put the vase on the narrow hall table used for keys, mail, spare coins and, at Christmastime, a Hummel nativity scene. She returned to the bench, rubbing her slacks down with her palms as she walked. "Those are beautiful. She'll love them."

"Excuse me for asking, but my mother didn't know to much. All we know is that Bea has been sick. I guess Mr. Edwin told my dad, who told my mom, who told me."

Mrs. Edwin was hesitant. She didn't know how much she should say and how much Bea should tell him herself, but he had been like a son for years, and seeing him again warmed her heart. "It's good to see you."

Ryan brightened. "I've missed you."

"I understand why you haven't been around, but that Kincaid boy meant nothing to Bea. They went on three dates and after the last one, she came home crying. Apparently, he took her to a party but ended up hanging out with some other girl while they were there. You would never treat her that way."

Feeling respectful, Ryan nodded.

"And you're getting more handsome by the day. How is that even possible? You look just like a young Elvis Presley. You've got those dreamy blue eyes and those…well, here I am embarrassing myself and probably you as well." She laughed at herself and he liked her for it.

"How's the dance studio?"

"Same old, same old. I only go in once a week lately, since Bea fell ill."

"What exactly—?"

"Do you know anything about rheumatoid arthritis?"

"That's an old-person thing where your bones hurt, right?"

"Well, it can strike young people too, even when you're in high school."

Ryan picked at the buttons on the cuffs of his striped Oxford shirt and listened.

"It's a disease that causes the body's immune system to attack its joints. She takes folic acid, hydrocodone, Oxycontin, Naproxin, prednisone, and muscle relaxers to manage the pain, but I have difficulty controlling how may pills she should be taking. She's been allocated a dozen Lortab, a dozen muscle relaxers, and two Oxycontin per day, but I think there have been days she's had far more than prescribed because I've found her passed out in her room more than once." Mrs. Edwin started stroking her arm in a self-soothing gesture before she moved on to her hair. She combed it with her fingers as she continued. "Remember how energetic she used to be? She's not that girl anymore."

Ryan felt like he'd been punched in the gut and said nothing.

Mrs. Edwin stopped stroking her hair and looked like she was about to cry.

"Now all she says is that she wants to die."

27

Brown eyes wide, chestnut hair hanging in sweaty strands, Logan watched and waited. The men seemed enraged by the state of the yard.

The first druggie punted a lightweight container a good twelve feet. "What the hell is this, an obstacle course?"

The second meth-addled man kicked a stack of boxes that tipped over and spilled.

"Bunch of shit," he muttered. The sirens grew louder. "We gotta go."

"No, we gotta get the kid! He saw us!"

The second man shook his head. "He doesn't know what he saw."

They argued as they left the backyard, punching and kicking boxes as they went. Logan counted to ten before he crawled back into his own yard and then went out into the middle of the street, yards from the tangle of trucks there to fight the blaze. The killers backed away from the smashed Chevelle and peeled away without a backward glance.

One of the firemen turned and saw Logan, standing alone in the middle of the road. In a daze, the boy clutched the deluxe limited edition Elvis album from 1957 as another fire engine roared down the street and navigated around Jarrod's beloved and now battered ride, siren blaring.

The fireman came and scooped Logan up into his arms. The boy's dirty gray long johns were damp; he had wet himself.

"You gotta get out of the street. Is that your house?"

Logan nodded.

As neighbors began to gather on front lawns, the firemen finished extinguishing the blaze. Logan glared at them. *What took you so long?*

"Who was inside? You have brothers? Sisters?"

Logan shook his head.

"Your mom?"

Logan nodded.

A nearby fireman waved to a paramedic on the scene. A team approached the house with a stretcher and disappeared through the dark, gaping hole that was once a front door.

"Your dad?"

Logan shook his head and wriggled to indicate he wanted to be put down. The fireman obliged, and Logan took the man's hand and led him over to the wrecked Chevelle. Jarrod lay behind the door on the driver's side, half in the car, half on the ground. He had taken a single shot to the head and several to the chest.

"Is that—is that your dad?"

Logan nodded. His lip trembled.

The fireman checked for a pulse and frowned. Logan knew what that meant from television shows he'd seen. He turned toward the house and watched as paramedics carried the remains of his mother out. She weighed more than three hundred pounds, and they labored to get her down the front steps. Logan wandered away from the fireman and went up to the stretcher. The paramedics paused and looked at him as he reached out to touch the sheet, the Elvis LP still clutched in his other hand.

"The kid. Get the kid," someone shouted.

Logan felt himself being hoisted up again.

28

Mrs. Edwin called after Ryan got home from school the very next day to tell him Bea wanted to see him, so he took a shower, put on a clean white dress shirt and khakis, grabbed his cell phone and a two-liter bottle of Diet Pepsi, and headed next door.

With formal solemnity, Mrs. Edwin let him in. The flowers had been cleared away from the foyer table, and the air conditioning seemed to be set high. It created an icy atmosphere at odds with the fact Mrs. Edwin wore a blue woolen sweater that had pilled along the arms and front. "I don't know whether to take this old sweater off or keep it on. I get hot, then I get cold, and then I get hot again."

Ryan knew about menopause and suspected Mrs. Edwin was going through hormonal changes, which he certainly didn't want to discuss. When she waved him toward the staircase, he nodded politely and headed up to Bea's room.

Her door was closed, so he knocked and waited.

"Come in." Her voice was slurry like his dad's, when he drank.

He turned the knob and pushed the door inward. The room was no longer decorated with Disney princesses; they had been supplanted. Clocks of every shape and size now filled the walls, which had been repainted an inviting peach. In bed, Bea was flipping through an issue of *Marie Claire*. When she saw Ryan, she let the magazine fall shut and laid it flat on her legs, which formed two straight rails beneath the thin floral coverlet. "How do you do it?" That was the first thing she said, and he didn't know what she meant.

"Get better looking every goddamn year?" she continued, when she saw his blank expression.

Ryan blushed and pointed to the chair at her white desk.

Bea nodded, so he went and sat down.

"You've seen me at school."

She waved her hand. "In passing."

"But you never look at me."

"You never look at me."

They sat there in silence while Ryan looked around the room. The flowers he'd brought were now on her dresser, which faced the foot of her bed. Ryan sniffed the air but couldn't detect any scent. Maybe they were too far away.

"I'm sorry."

Bea frowned. "Sorry we haven't talked since junior high?"

Ryan shrugged and pulled at his collar to straighten it. "Kincaid."

"Kincaid means nothing. Have you seen me with him at all? Come on, Ryan, it's been years. Have you seen me date anyone?"

"No."

"Make out with anyone in the halls?"

He shook his head, chastened.

"Did you know I was diagnosed with rheumatoid arthritis when I was a freshman? That I've had this sucky disease for two years now?"

Ryan's throat closed. He couldn't speak. She was the best girl he had ever known. The only girl he had ever kissed or held hands with. And that one night, he had felt so betrayed he never wanted to see her again.

"Now that you know I'm sick, though," she said, "you feel sorry for me."

"I am." He paused. "Sorry you're sick."

She let out a sudden, explosive laugh that caused him to jump. "Oh, it's fine, it's fine. The drugs are great."

Ryan knew her well enough to know she was bluffing. He came over and sat on her bed. He reached out for her hand. She looked at him, startled, and then placed her hand in his upturned palm. He interlaced their fingers and gave her hand a firm squeeze.

"Tell me about it."

Bea burst into big, blubbery tears that caused her nose to run. She had held so much in for so long and hadn't let anyone in. Hadn't had him. Now he held her close, not minding the tears and the snot dampening his shoulder. He would hold her as long as it took, and he would not let go. Finally, the tears abated, and Bea stared up at him, her blue eyes luminous.

He stroked her hair back from her face. They were both sixteen, and their childhood affection had taken a sharp turn into a sexual realm. Her sandy blonde curls had grown past her shoulders to the middle of her back, and oftentimes now she let her hair hang free instead of tying it back or up. He tilted her chin upward and gave her a long, deep kiss far different from the innocent pecks he'd dared to give her in junior high. She was a woman now, and her breasts were full. He cupped one in his hand and felt giddy, and then, just as suddenly, he dropped his hand. She was sick. He shouldn't be thinking about sex. "Tell me about it."

She looked at him, confused by his pulling back.

He grinned. "We have plenty of time later to catch up in other departments. I want to know exactly what you're going through."

Bea's mother had always told her that Ryan was mature beyond his years, and now she thought she understood. Most boys wanted to dive right into heavy petting. Ryan was different; he cared about her heart. She stared up at the canopy over her bed, an expanse of frilly ruffles that made her feel as if they were sitting beneath a peach sky.

"I'm in pain all the time. My bones hurt so badly in my legs and arms, I just want to scream. Today I've taken plenty of meds, so I can hold your hand without wanting to rip your head off. But look." She rolled up the sleeve of her camouflage patterned thermal shirt and showed him a series of bumps. Those are rheumatoid nodules. Aren't they gross?"

She glanced at him and he shook his head that, no, they weren't.

"I get up in the morning and I can barely move I'm so stiff. I'm tired all the time. My head is always hot. Here, feel my head."

She took his free hand and pressed it against her forehead, and Ryan thought she felt warm.

"And I don't feel like eating." She tossed the magazine off her lap and pulled down the covers so he could see her waistline.

"I don't think you look bad at all."

"Eating makes me sick. When I try to hold a pen, my fingers cramp up because my knuckles ache so badly. And look." She yanked the coverlet down so she could pull her legs out. "Look at my feet. I can't bend my toes they're so stiff. It's like I'm freaking ninety years old. My hips hurt, my shoulders hurt, my knees hurt, my ankles hurt, and my elbows hurt. Crap, even my face hurts."

Ryan couldn't hold himself back. He needed to kiss her again.

He leaned forward and pressed his lips against hers. "Does this hurt?"

"No," she giggled. "Not so much."

29

Uncle Wendall drove back to Las Vegas slowly, steering the Cadillac like a luxury boat up the I-15 North toward Barstow, eventually crossing into Nevada, which looked like a deserted wasteland of cacti, tumbleweeds, dirt, rocks, and billboards assuring the road-weary that Sin City had rooms ready for them. Compared to the bustle of Santa Monica, the route looked like a nuclear blast had cleared the area of all life save that at truck stops, where burly drivers stopped for chili and burgers, and rest stops, where tired travelers sorted through trinkets and bought gallons of soda, cups of burned coffee, candy bars, and potato chips. It was early evening, and the windows were down as they drove. Logan sat beside his uncle, unable to talk, still clutching the *Elvis' Christmas Album* like a blankie.

Going through his sister's destroyed home had left Wendall dispirited. Instead of charred rooms filled with blackened furniture, emergency personnel offered him large rubber boots two sizes too large so he could wade through the premises. Each room looked like the site of an ongoing archaeological dig, with piles of ashes and the occasional half-burnt item, the ruins piled knee high even as it was reduced to gossamer grayness. Ash swirled around him as he poked stacks with a charred yardstick. The upper strata seemed to be newer items, circa the mid-nineties, and the second layer seemed to contain items from the eighties, including some of Logan's baby clothing and toys. Beneath that, there were items from the seventies, sixties, and fifties, many of them belonging to MawMaw that Ramona had been unable to part with.

His sister's life lay before him in slabs that could be peeled away, and they told the tale of mental illness and hoarding, the sickness of too much stuff. He tossed the yardstick he had been excavating with and a cloud of ash filled the room like gray snow. He wanted to sit down and cry, but he had to be strong for the child. Social workers said Logan had stopped talking the night his parents died. It was one of those deeply concerned women who had remembered Ramona had a brother, because he was mentioned by name the day Angela confronted Ramona and Jarrod in their cluttered backyard.

"This is Wendall's fault, isn't it?"
"I'm sorry, ma'am. Wendall?"
"My brother! My brother called you!"

After ascertaining that Ramona's maiden name was Johns, they located only one Wendall Johns in the United States, a retired fertility specialist who lived in Las Vegas, and gave him a call. He was there within six hours to claim his nephew and sign the necessary paperwork granting him permanent custody of the boy he'd always felt sorry for.

Wendall's ambition had receded with the passing years. After he had bankrolled enough green to retire in comfort, he closed the fertility clinic on Harmon and moved to a gated community a few miles off the strip. His backyard faced the back nine of an eighteen-hole golf course, and he played at eight every Tuesday, Thursday, and Saturday with three pals he also played poker with every Monday and Wednesday night. Sunday was his day of rest. Instead of going to church, he got several newspapers, made a pot of coffee, stretched out on his living room chaise in front of the fireplace, and flipped through every page of every paper, sometimes stopping to read a headline, occasionally stopping to peruse a story.

Wendall looked over at the malnourished boy who sat so far away, he was pressed against the passenger door. Bruises dotted his arms and bare legs like leopard spots. He didn't want to think about how Logan had gotten them. Recalling the last time he'd seen him, he began to sing. "This old man, he played one, he played knick-knack on my thumb, with a knick-knack

The New Elvis

paddy-whack, give a dog a bone, this old man came rolling home."

Logan didn't budge.

"This old man, he played two, he played knick-knack on my shoe, with a knick-knack paddy-whack, give a dog a bone, this old man came rolling home."

Logan stirred a bit on the seat, like he needed to go to the bathroom but couldn't or wouldn't ask.

"You need me to stop?"

Logan turned and met his uncle's open, blue-eyed gaze with his own dark, haunted eyes. He nodded.

Wendall pointed at a sign fifty yards in the distance. "Good timing. There's a stop in five miles. That's about five minutes. Can you hold it that long?"

Again, Logan nodded, grateful that his uncle was taking care of him. He remembered the song, remembered the warm feeling he'd had the day they played with the big plastic ball on the front lawn, and remembered the old Cadillac. This new one smelled good and looked like shiny blueberries, if blueberries could shine. Somehow, he doubted it. Fruit didn't shine unless you waxed it, like Mrs. Henn, who kept a big golden bowl of fake apples and pears on her dining room table, and he was certain, what with blueberries being so small, it would take at least an hour to wax a whole bowlful.

His uncle smelled like coconuts, so he must still be wearing the same tropical cologne. He seemed like the kind of man who, when he liked something, he stuck with it. Not like his mom, who bought a fragrant beauty product, tried it, put it in a box, and then bought the next one, hoping she'd like it more.

As his uncle pulled in at the rest stop, Logan looked down at the red *Elvis' Christmas Album* in his lap. It was the one thing worth saving from his house. MawMaw and his mother had always been happy listening to Elvis as they played cards. When they were happy, they didn't yell or tell him what to do. They were in their own bubble of lady-talk, their chatter a counterpoint to Elvis' smooth singing voice.

"You going to stare at that album all night or are you gonna come with me?" Wendall didn't sound angry. He stood at the open passenger door and waited patiently for Logan's attention. Logan looked up, slid off the seat, and followed his uncle, still carrying the album. Wendall noticed but said nothing. The boy had been through more than a child should, and if he wanted to carry an album, so be it.

They took a leak and washed their hands in companionable silence, then headed back to the car. Wendall held the door open on the passenger side for the boy as he slid back in, then closed it gently behind him before heading over to the driver's side.

Logan stared at Uncle Coconuts as he got behind the wheel. He wasn't too fat and he wasn't too thin. He was in-betweenish, like his dark hair, which was part gray and part brown. He had a receding hairline, a smooth forehead, and a tanned face with bright eyes, an ordinary nose, and a straight thin line for lips. His clothes looked like what his friends' dads wore. Dark pants and shoes, an open-collared shirt, a jacket that zipped up the front. His friends' dads had clean hands and nice wristwatches, just like him. Their hair was always neatly combed, and they never seemed to get irritated.

Wendall glanced over. Logan pretended he hadn't been staring at him. His eyes quickly shifted to the dashboard, to the illuminated dials and buttons. There were more miles ahead, all predictable for Wendall, who had driven the route before. What was less predictable was how the boy would take to life in Las Vegas, in his old-man pad, with few kids around. He would, as the social workers warned him, just have to take it one day at a time.

30

Ryan and Bea were in the middle of a lingering kiss when the cell phone in Ryan's pocket rang.

Bea pulled back. "Is that a phone in your pocket, or are you—?"

They both laughed. Ryan untangled his hand from Bea's long hair and dug into his front pocket. He looked up, frowning. "My dad."

"Probably sold a house and wants you to be as excited about it as he is."

Ryan dialed his father's cell.

"Guess what?" Gene's voice was so loud Bea could hear him without any trouble.

"What?"

"Your grandparents are here!"

Ryan was puzzled. "I thought they lived in Thailand."

"They did. They do. They came back for a visit."

"After twenty years?"

"Well, they like it over there. It took them a while to get motivated to take a trip. They're old, you know. People slow down."

"When do I meet them?"

"Your mom is cooking dinner for us right now. You're with Bea?"

Ryan leaned over and kissed her ear. "Yep."

"How is she?"

"We can talk about that when I get there."

"Well, get a move on, son. Your grandparents aren't getting any younger."

Ryan sat up on Bea's bed and looked around at the clocks. A quarter past five, a quarter past five, a quarter past five. They all kept perfect time.

He slid off the bed. "I gotta go."

"Your grandparents are here?"

"Yeah. Never met 'em."

"Well, good luck." She winced as she rose from the bed. "It's time for me to knock myself out for a while anyway."

Ryan thought Bea would walk him to the door, but she stopped at her bureau and opened the top drawer. It was full of fat vials from the pharmacy. She took a bottle, unscrewed the cap, and dropped two oblong white tablets into her palm.

"What's that?"

"Vicodin."

Of the litany of drugs Bea's mom had listed off the top of her head that her daughter was taking, Ryan hadn't remembered Vicodin being included in the rundown. Then again, she was taking so many different pills it would be hard to remember them all.

31

Uncle Wendall's home was magnificent, and Logan had his own room at the top of the sweeping staircase that led downstairs to the living room. His uncle had a lady friend named Nancy, who came over twice a week to visit but never stayed long, and she often spent time alone with Logan, sitting with him as he played, silently, on the carpet in his lavish room.

"Is there anything you need?" Nancy asked him.

She had helped him shop for new clothing at Macy's, where he'd point at what he wanted, which she'd take with him to the dressing room, where she would wait patiently to see if what he picked fit him or if they'd need a different size. He was also taking baths every night before bed now, and he had twenty pairs of pajamas, mostly all superhero-themed.

Before bedtime, he would kneel next to his new, large bed covered with an X-Men spread, and put his forehead down on his fists, his fingers laced together. He would pray for his mother and father, pray that he wouldn't have nightmares about the bad men, and pray that he would get his voice back so he could go to school like a normal kid.

Then, after his uncle tucked him in, he would point to the turntable on the dresser. Uncle Wendall would go over, lift the lid, turn the player on, drop the needle, and, to the faint strains of *Elvis' Christmas Album*, Logan would drift off to sleep.

When the local elementary school found out that Logan was unwilling or unable to talk, they decided he had selective mutism and told Uncle Wendall to take him to a specialist, who sat with him but never made any progress.

The therapist would talk about anything that was on his mind, which never interested Logan. One day, at the door, the therapist told Uncle Wendall that he had heard of a case where a young man stopped talking because he had a speech impediment that made him reluctant to talk because of the teasing he'd received. His mother was abusive, making him feel like whatever he had to contribute to a conversation was worthless. He hadn't spoken for ten years at the time he was brought in for therapy. They uncovered some of his personal writings, where he referred to IPA, the International Phonetic Alphabetic, representing only those qualities of speech in spoken language. It was proof to the doctor that the young man could speak but chose not to.

"He was older than your nephew, but the challenge is similar."

Uncle Wendall told the doctor that Logan had never had a speech impediment and that, while his mother had been difficult, he believed the bond between Logan and his mother had been a close one, that Logan saw himself as important in her life, helpful in the face of her emotional and physical difficulties.

"Maybe he feels guilty he couldn't save her," the doctor posited.

Wendall shook his head. "I think he knows that the fire wasn't his fault."

"Maybe he's experiencing survivor's guilt."

Wendall studied Logan carefully. Clean cut, with his hair freshly clipped and combed at the barbershop, he barely resembled the raggedy kid he had rescued. "I just don't know."

"Try to get him interested in something," the doctor urged. "Find out what he likes, what he's good at. Do anything you can to lessen his anxiety. Find something he can throw himself into and excel at."

Though Wendall was retired and liked his schedule of golf games and poker just fine, he picked up the necessary textbooks from the school district and began to home school Logan. He also tried to teach him how to play poker, sitting him down at the card table after one of his Wednesday night games to show him various hands.

Placing the Ace of diamonds and the Queen of spades together, followed by the Queen of diamonds and the King of spades, followed by the ten of spades and the nine of diamonds, he asked Logan which hand would be strongest, pre-flop, in a game of Texas Hold'em.

Logan shrugged, and Wendall pointed at the first pair. "Ace high starts off strong."

Then Wendall laid down the flop: the seven of hearts, the seven of spades, and the three of spades. "Okay, how about now?"

Logan didn't know.

Wendall pointed to the first pair again. "Ace, Queen continues to lead. Okay, now here's the turn card."

He flipped over the nine of clubs and looked at Logan expectantly, but Logan wasn't catching on.

"Ten, nine is now in the lead," Wendall told him, placing the river card on the table. It was the Queen of clubs. "How about now?"

Logan shrugged.

"Ace, Queen. Highest two pair and the Ace kicker takes it."

Everything about Logan's body language told Wendall he was bored. Wendall scooped up the cards and smiled. "Maybe some other time."

Life went on that way for years, as Wendall continued to test and see where Logan's interests might lie, as he continued to guide Logan through his studies, to the point where Logan would soon be ready to get his high school equivalency certificate. Over the years, the only addition to the household was a Siamese cat named Professor X, who was as loud as Logan was silent. Nancy continued to come around with regularity, and one day, she brought Logan a Microsoft Tablet PC so he could carry it around and write notes to them.

Then, one Sunday, close to one in the afternoon, just as Wendall finished his several newspapers, dropping them onto the carpet section by section as he finished them, something curious happened.

Logan entered the living room with a pair of scissors and sat down on the rug at his uncle's feet. He took the entertainment sections from the *New York Times*, the *Los Angeles Times*, the *San Francisco Chronicle*, and the *Las Vegas Review-Journal*, cut out the main photos and stories, and rearranged them carefully to form an amalgamated spread that was pleasing to the eye.

Uncle Wendall stood up and looked it over. Logan had spaced the stories and photos out into a tableaux that was well balanced and effective. 2004 was winding to a close, so the entertainment news was a combination of events that had happened earlier in the year and more recently. Stories on Britney Spears' brief marriage to Jason Alexander, J.Lo and Ben Affleck's breakup, Janet Jackson's Super Bowl XXXVIII's halftime show performance snafu with Justin Timberlake, Arnold Schwarzenegger's appointment as the new governor of California, and the success of the new ABC show *Desperate Housewives* were all featured in Logan's spread.

Wendall knelt down and rested his arm across Logan's shoulders. "I see a few things going on here. You've got a killer eye for layout, you like entertainment, and it's time for me to get you a few layout and design programs for your computer."

Logan grinned and impulsively hugged his uncle, and when they broke from their embrace, it was impossible to tell which one of them was more surprised.

32

Zella had redecorated the front of the house earlier that year, and the focal point in the living room was now a sprawling, modern, white leather sectional, with seating for twelve that could be repositioned as she saw fit. When Ryan came home that day, the couch was arranged around a chrome-legged walnut matte table placed in the center of a Gandia Blasco hand-tufted that fit the entire room like a glove, ending six inches from the baseboards, its earth-tone stripes intermixed with turquoise, the color Zella chose for room accent pieces, throw pillows, and lamps.

Ryan tucked his white dress shirt into his khakis and took a swig from his bottle of Diet Pepsi before he opened the front door. Seated together in the middle of the sectional were his father's parents. His grandfather was a withered version of Gene, with sagging jowls, spindly arms, and stick-like legs. His grandmother was top-heavy and her frilly blouse covered her ample bosom and stomach like a frothy bib. She wore a thick skirt of nubbly fabric in a dusty rose that matched the splotches of rouge she'd dabbed on her cheeks. She had gone white-haired, while her husband had gone gray.

Ryan's parents stood in the entranceway to the dining room, watching their son's reaction to his grandparents and Gene's parents' reaction to their son. Everyone seemed frozen as they gazed at each other. Finally, Gene broke the ice. He went and put his arm around his Ryan's shoulder and steered him toward the couch. George and Katherine Wyatt rose and gave their grandson a hug. Ryan backed up, hit the coffee table, recovered, and took a seat adjacent to them. Grandma Katherine reached out and tapped the baby photo album on the table in front of them.

Ryan blushed. It was filled with pictures of him. His first meal eaten by himself with a spoon, orange squash on his cheeks and lips. His first ride in his doorway bouncy swing, his legs dangling from the seat, his feet inches above the ground. His first Halloween, dressed as Wolverine, flashing a fistful of plastic claws. His first Christmas, surrounded by squishy rubber blocks, his mother in the background, beaming. The school plays, when he was older, performing at the school. Bea, with a frown on her face, bent over the sandbox while he built a hill for his Matchbox cars to drive up. His first school dance, again with Bea, both of them unwilling to smile for the camera, wanting to appear grown-up and serious.

Grandma Katherine gazed across the room. "You look a bit like her," she said, referring to Zella.

"Him, not so much," Grandpa George added.

"Well, of course the boy doesn't look like Eugene. He's—"

Gene rushed over to the couch, intent on interrupting. "Mom, that's okay."

"What, he doesn't know?"

Ryan looked around the room at them. The air was still. No one spoke. Then, just as suddenly, Gene began to babble, determined to push past the moment.

"Hey, Ryan, remember Michael Knight-Lewis? We showed him that house where Nana went for a swim? He didn't want that one, but I showed him another one on Victoria Point. Four bedrooms, four baths, seven and a half million. Loads of pine trees on the property, no public beach access, so you're buying your own piece of the Pacific. It has a deck on the second level, with the bedrooms downstairs. You take a shower in the upstairs bath, and I kid you not, you're looking at the side of a cliff. Stairs go right down to the beach from the deck. A real surf spot."

Zella came over to the couch but didn't sit. "Gene, I'm sure Ryan would rather hear about your parents' adventures in Thailand." She looked at Ryan pointedly. "Don't you wonder what it would be to live there for twenty years?"

Ryan cleared his throat, ready to ask his grandparents a question.

Gene rolled on. "Well, Michael didn't like that house either, so I showed him a third one in Ramirez Canyon. Eleven acres, eight and a half million, five thousand square feet. It has a family area right off the side of the kitchen, which is something he really wanted, and—get this—the entire first floor was done in oak from a reclaimed barn in Oklahoma. Really gave the place character."

Ryan watched his mother leave the room. Gene didn't notice. He was locked in on his parents, trying to impress on them what a successful realtor he'd become. Quietly, Ryan got up and followed his mother. She was in the kitchen, trying to read the thermometer stuck in the browning turkey.

"Mom?"

She turned to look at him and then looked away, unable to hold his gaze.

"Dad's not my father?"

"Of course he's your father. He raised you, didn't he?"

Ryan came over and stood next to her. "I mean, my *real* father."

Zella pursed her lips. "I'm not sure this is the right time to—"

"They know and I don't? Everybody knows but me? I'm supposed to sit through a dinner with my grandparents and—"

Zella cringed. "Maybe we can talk about this later. With your father."

"Oh, sure. We've waited my entire life. What does a few more hours matter?"

He left his mother hovering over the turkey, her face shaded by a veil of dark hair that had fallen forward. He started to go back into the living room and then stopped. The conversation in the living room had shifted back to him.

"He looks like a little Elvis," Grandma Katherine was saying.

"Straight off *The Ed Sullivan Show*," Grandpa George agreed.

"Do you think she got the, uh," Grandma Katherine searched for a polite word, "*donation* from an Elvis impersonator?"

"Could be," Gene said. "There are plenty of them in Vegas."

"But she never found out who?" Grandpa George asked.

"She was never told who the donor was," Gene replied. "This doctor she went to, Wendall Johns, he was a real private guy. One hundred percent confidential."

33

While Bea lay on the left side of her bed, knitting the longest scarf in the world, Ryan lay on the right with his left hand slightly extended toward the open MacBook placed between them. The TV that had been set up in Bea's room not long after she was diagnosed with RA was turned on, and the movie *Almost Elvis: Elvis Impersonators and Their Quest for the Crown* filled the screen. Ryan had placed a pad of paper and a pen near the right-side edge of the bed and was prepared to take notes.

After the opening montage of Elvis impersonators, the screen filled with the following words: "Every year, thousands of Elvis impersonators compete in regional contests all across America. Those who win qualify for a berth to the Super Bowl of all Elvis contests: the Images of Elvis World Championships in Memphis, Tennessee."

Ryan straightened the pillow behind his head and grabbed a second one so he could prop himself up better.

A sign in front of a building in South Bend, Indiana, listed a pancake breakfast on the 21st, a sock hop on the 26th, and an Elvis contest on the 27th. Inside the building, men were busy taping the floor and hanging up decorative sheets on the walls in preparation for the Midwest regional qualifier events. At a table, cassette tapes and index cards were in the process of being sorted. An Elvis impersonator laced up the front of his jumpsuit, and a man fiddled with a soundboard while the Elvis impersonator in the folding chair next to him wrote something down.

Johnny Thompson spoke first, complaining about people yanking on his sideburns to see if they were real. Then, Quentin Flagg thanked someone who told him he looked awesome with a "thank you very much." Next, Steve Sogura told people that he knew when he grew his sideburns out and dyed his hair, he was setting himself up for criticism. Robert Washington admitted he wasn't likely to become rich and famous by impersonating Elvis, but he considered it a dream come true. Next, Doug Church checked to make sure his sideburns were even. Rich Andrews fixed his Elvis 'do when he noticed a reflective surface he could see himself in. A jumpsuit-clad Irv Cass complained that he'd put on a bit of weight. And one judge mentioned that the first thing he looked for was the voice.

While Irv Cass ate breakfast with family and friends, he mentioned that the Elvis contest, Images of Elvis, was the biggest Elvis impersonation contest in the world. Meanwhile, in Indiana, Quentin Flagg delivered newspapers on his bicycle.

Ryan leaned forward as if to see the screen better. "That guy is about our age. When was this movie made?"

Bea stuck the tips of her knitting needles into a ball of cornflower blue yarn and performed a Google search on the laptop. "2000. So, if that kid was a teenager then, he's—"

"Too young to be my dad."

As the documentary continued, Quentin's dad said that, just as the Colonel told Elvis his talent was worth a million dollars and he was going to get Elvis a million dollars, he wanted to do that for his own son.

"Oh, my God." Bea made a face, pulled her knitting needles out of the thick ball of yarn, and grabbed her sports bottle, three-quarters full of water. "Can you imagine having a stage mom or dad like that, managing your career as an Elvis impersonator?"

Ryan mimicked Gene. "I know we've got to get to Memphis, Ry. Just let me stop in Malibu and check on that beachfront property first."

Bea nearly choked with laughter as she took a sip. "And what about your mom?"

Ry cleared his throat and, in a higher pitch, said, "I know you're a good Elvis impersonator, Ryan, but don't you think your act would be better if you incorporated a few magic tricks?"

Bea recapped her bottle and slid out of bed. Stiffly, she moved to the bureau, where she kept her meds. She uncapped a few vials, slipped a few pills into her mouth, and minced back to bed as slowly as if she were eighty years old.

"Jeez, Bea, if you're this creaky now, what's going to happen when you get old?"

"I'm not going to get old," she retorted. "I'm going to die young and beautiful."

"What about our wedding? I thought we were gonna have an Elvis impersonator marry us in Vegas."

Bea smiled. "That's two years away. If I die in ten, I'll still be young and beautiful."

She slid back onto the bed and Ryan leaned over to kiss her on the lips, but she pulled back. He'd forgotten she'd put pills in her mouth. She held up an index finger, grabbed her water bottle, uncapped it, and took a swig. Then she kissed him, slowly, warmly. Ryan thought she tasted like honey. When Bea pulled away, she had a thoughtful look on her face. "Do you think we're ever going to find your real father?"

"I hope so."

She glanced back at the TV screen. "Think it's one of these Elvis contestants?"

"One of them," Ryan said, "or maybe someone who's played Elvis in a movie. But to be an impersonator, you've got to have a voice."

"Well, we know you didn't get your singing talent from Zella or Gene, so you're right. It's probably one of these guys who can really belt out a song."

34

Bea was beneath her coverlet, her bony knees forming tents, while Ryan was on top, propped in a pile of pillows so he could see the TV. Twirling her blond curls in her fingers, Bea looked at Ryan, dreamy-eyed. "How many kids do you want to have?"

"Three," Ryan said, without thinking.

"Three would be nice," she murmured, snuggling close.

"Wait a minute. I thought you were going to die young."

"Well, sure," she laughed. "I'm going to pop the kids out, one a year, starting with the year after we're married in Vegas by the Elvis impersonator, and then I'm going to die, and you're going to be the best single parent on earth, and win all kinds of awards, and all the moms in the PTA are going to have crushes on you."

"Awards for what?" Ryan looked at the clocks of every shape and size filling Bea's peach walls and realized how aware of time she was. He took off his Nikes and slid beneath the coverlet. It was four-thirty. He had at least an hour before Zella would call him on his cell and make him come home for dinner. She was no longer "Mom," and his dad had become simply "Gene." The shift in how he saw them occurred the very moment his mother stood in their kitchen and wouldn't meet his gaze.

Bea buried her face in his neck. "I had the weirdest dream last night. There was this turtle in a flat-bottomed dish filled with water, but it didn't have a shell. It wanted other creatures to stick pins in it. I didn't see what was doing the sticking, but the pins were stuck in the turtle. Then someone came and tried to take the pins out of the turtle, but while the person was removing them, the turtle opened its craw, ran toward a sharp object protruding from the inside of its bowl, and impaled itself."

"Have you ever had this dream before?"

Bea shook her head and some of her hair got into Ryan's mouth. He removed it from his lips and kissed her forehead before sitting back up, causing her to slip sideways.

They now faced each other. "What do you think it means?"

"I'll think about it and let you know, but it sounds like the kind of crazy dream that doesn't mean anything."

Bea nodded, satisfied. "I was thinking more about *Elvis: The Miniseries*, and I went back after you left yesterday and watched every move Jonathan Rhys Meyers made. You guys look the same, move the same, and sound the same. Do you think you could be brothers? He's only eleven years older than you are."

"Yeah, but he was born in Dublin. What are the odds a sperm bank sends its juice to Ireland?"

"Maybe his parents were here, then moved there, and then moved back."

Ryan was dubious. "He has three younger brothers, all accounted for. It's doubtful they wouldn't know about me or need help from a fertility clinic to have me. Sounds like all four kids were regular births."

"He spent time in an orphanage, though. Maybe we don't have the whole story."

Ryan sighed, giving up on that idea. "What are we going to watch today?"

They had been watching movies in her bed for months, had celebrated their seventeenth birthdays without fanfare, and were still no closer to finding out who Ryan's real dad was.

Bea hit the remote and the next Elvis-themed movie began. This one was called *Elvis Has Left The Building*, and it had a roster of impressive stars.

"Read the intro," Bea begged as words filled the screen. "I don't want to get up and find my glasses."

"Elvis Presley died in August 1977. At the time of his death, there were three known Elvis impersonators. Today, there are over 50,000. If that figure continues to grow at the present rate, by the year 2012, one out of every four people on the planet will be an Elvis impersonator. In the face of this potential threat to world security, a miracle occurred...and her name was Harmony Jones."

Bea giggled and they settled in to watch the show. It opened with actor Gil McKinney, driving his trademark pink Cadillac, giving a little blond girl a ride home. The year on the screen read "1950," and he was singing *Down By The Riverside*. The girl asked Elvis how she could thank him for the ride, and he told her that maybe someday she'd do something special for him. Flashing forward to the present day, Harmony was driving her own pink Caddy, selling Pink Lady cosmetics, knowing Elvis would guide her wherever she went. In the course of the movie, Harmony found herself in the company of Elvis impersonators, all of whom died in freak accidents, culminating in the largest calamity of all, when a roof at a convention center collapsed from the weight of all the Elvis impersonators standing on it, watching the skies, looking for a sign from The King.

"So the favor Harmony did for Elvis was killing off all the Elvis impersonators," Ryan surmised as Bea clicked the remote and the screen went dark. "I don't think I liked that movie. Plus, no one in it could be my dad."

"Are you sure? Go through it for me."

"Real Elvis Gil McKinney was born in '79, so he could be my brother but not my dad. The director, Joel Zwick, who played Squashed Elvis, could be my dad, but he's pretty famous and we don't know if he can sing. Mailbox Elvis was played by Tom Hanks, and the likelihood of Hanks donating sperm to a fertility clinic is remote. Plus, we don't know if he can sing. Hole-in-the-head Elvis is David Leisure. He's too much of an oddball to be a serious dad candidate. Then you've got Burning Elvis, played by Richard Kind, who's just a sitcom guy."

Bea sighed. "So let's go over the Elvises in the other movies."

"We've been through them all. Jim Belushi as Elvis in *Easy Six*? No. Henry Herrera as Elvis in *Rancho Cucamonga*? No. Michael de la Force from *Elvis & June: A Love Story*? No. Bruce Campbell in *Bubba Ho-Tep*? Don't make me laugh."

"Well, it was a funny movie."

"Any one of the guys in *3000 Miles to Graceland*? No. Shawn Wayne Klush from *Shake, Rattle and Roll: An American Love Story*? Nope. Harvey Keitel from *Finding Graceland*? Never. Pieter Kuijpers from *Elvis Lives!*? No. You can go all the way back to Kurt Russell, and my dad is *not* Colonel Jack O'Neil from *Stargate*."

"Okay, okay. So maybe we have to go about things differently."

Ryan started to put his Nikes back on. "We've just about run out of Elvis movies anyway. Maybe..." He stopped, fixated on one of the many clocks over Bea's white desk. "No, that would be crazy."

"What?"

"When my grandparents came over for dinner, my dad mentioned my mom's doctor in Vegas. He said his name was Wendall Johns."

35

Because their friend Noah was eighteen and had a car, Bea and Ryan convinced him to take a weekend road trip with them, using the cover story that they were off to visit a fellow senior who had to move in the middle of the school year because his dad was transferred at work. Since Zella liked to keep mementos, it had only taken Ryan a month of Saturdays to find the card with Dr. Wendall Johns' business address and phone number on it, paper-clipped inside a tiny 1988 calendar that was stapled on the fold.

In Vegas, a woman sat on the second-story porch of the condo she shared with her husband and two young daughters, as Ramona had done so long ago. She was thin, with a head of wispy angel hair, and her girls were sitting at her feet, playing a game of checkers, when Noah, Bea, and Ryan pulled up in Noah's red Mustang. Noah parked at the curb, and they got out, confused by what they saw. The former fertility clinic had been turned into a tanning salon, plastered with posters of scantily clad men and women with ripped, tanned bodies.

Bea's sweet but weary voice floated up to the woman on the porch. "Are you sure this is the right address?"

The dark-haired boy who looked like Elvis studied the business card he withdrew from his wallet. "This is it."

The woman on the porch stood up, stepped over her daughters' game in progress, and moved to the railing. "What are you looking for?"

The trio looked up, and the dark-haired boy spoke. "Las Vegas Fertility Associates."

The woman's angel hair floated around her face like gauze. "That place hasn't been here for years."

"What about Dr. Wendall Johns?"

"That's the guy who ran the place. He retired. Moved to Rolling Hills Estates, over by the golf course. I think the 'Rolling Hills' part comes from the fact that to buy a place there, you've got to be rolling in hills of cash."

The teenagers laughed politely, and didn't bother to get directions. Instead, they went back to the car, and the angel-haired lady watched as Ryan helped Bea get into the back seat. The woman wondered what was wrong with the girl and felt sorry for her.

"King me!" one of the girls on the porch shouted.

Ryan turned back and looked at the porch, then got in the front seat beside Noah. The sun was beginning to set, amidst ribbons of lavender and blue, as the trio located Rolling Hills and were given directions to Dr. Johns' house.

Ryan punched the doorbell three times, and then waited.

Inside, Logan debated whether or not to answer the door. His uncle had gone out for an early dinner with Nancy, so he was alone. He paced, holding Professor X, who finally meowed loudly. He looked down at him and smiled. Maybe it wouldn't hurt to take a peek.

The hinges on the door didn't squeak, but the door opened so slowly, Bea felt a chill run down her spine. The four teenagers stared at each other for a moment before Ryan spoke up. "Hi, uh, does Dr. Johns live here?"

Logan stared at Ryan. Though he was dressed in jeans and a blue hoodie, he looked exactly like Elvis had back in the fifties. He nodded at them.

Ryan exhaled. "Oh, good. Is he here?"

Logan shook his head.

"What's the matter?" Noah asked. "Did you lose your voice?"

Embarrassed, Logan flushed scarlet and shook his head.

Bea nudged him in the ribs. "Shut up, Noah. He's probably mute."

Logan shook his head at the pretty girl and then held up a finger. He went and got his tablet and typed a message. When he was done, he held it up to the screen door, but they couldn't read it. Logan snapped on the porch light, but it didn't help. Taking a chance, Logan unlatched the screen, stood back, and waved them in.

"Thanks, man," Ryan said.

They were only a few feet into the foyer area. Logan handed Ryan the tablet as the Siamese cat circled their legs. Bea took her time and lowered her wracked frame into a crouch so she could see the cat better. She looked up at Logan. "What a beautiful cat! What's his name?"

The dark-eyed boy nervously tucked a wave of chestnut hair behind his right ear and shook his head.

Bea clapped a hand over her mouth. "Sorry. I forgot."

My uncle isn't here right now, Ryan read aloud.

He typed a message and handed the tablet back to Logan.

Do you know if he kept records from when he ran the clinic? Logan read the note, shook his head, and passed the tablet back to Ryan. He knew about his uncle's fertility clinic and he had seen boxes of tapes and logs in his uncle's study, but he'd never been interested in checking them out. He surmised Ryan wanted to know about his real father.

Noah was impatient. "Why don't we go to the show at Bar Fifty-Six like you wanted and come back later?"

Logan perked up and stood taller. Bar Fifty-Six was a new lounge tucked a block off the strip, behind The Mirage. Every night without fail—including holidays—they had a show featuring Elvis impersonators who specifically concentrated on 1956, the year Elvis made it big. The show ran an hour, and afterwards, they held an hour of Elvis karaoke, when audience members were invited to come up and sing Elvis songs for the crowd. Logan had wanted to go there ever since it opened.

Ryan noticed that Logan was interested, just as he himself was interested in securing an opportunity to meet the doctor. "You want to come with us, and then we'll bring you back? Maybe your uncle will be home by then."

Logan couldn't help himself. He nodded vigorously, ran to grab a jacket, scribbled a hasty note he stuck to the fridge with a magnet, and rejoined them in the foyer. He had his own set of house keys that he'd never used, which were now in his pocket on a tiny gold ring. These kids seemed to like him, and they didn't seem to mind his silence. The idea of getting out of the house and going to a club was so intoxicating he was about to faint, but he kept putting one foot in front of the other and managed to make it out the door behind them.

36

It was a night none of the teenagers would ever forget. Bar Fifty-Six, a circular stucco building the color and texture of oatmeal, had a simple blue neon sign over the front double-door entrance, but inside, the theatre was dressed in rich, sumptuous black velvet, from the cushy seats to the drapes onstage. The bar in the lobby was well stocked, and Noah had no trouble getting four Yuengling Traditional Lagers—no glasses, thanks—for the group, but Logan shook his head when he saw the bottles, so Noah drank two, and Ryan and Bea had the others. They took took seats in the third row, behind two blue-haired ladies and an octogenarian with a glammed-up blond half his age.

Seated on the left in an aisle seat, Noah leaned toward Ryan. "There was a card in the lobby that said they showcase songs from 1956 through 1957, so I guess that gives you an extra year of material to work with."

Ryan was surprised. "Who said I was going to sing?"

Seated on Ryan's right, Bea laughed. "That's why we're here, isn't it?"

On Bea's right, Logan beamed. Including the year 1957 meant that *Elvis' Christmas Album* would be part of the mix. He pulled out his tablet, typed a note for Ryan, and passed it to him.

Ryan squinted at the tablet in the dim light. *Sing White Christmas.*

He nodded in Logan's direction and passed the tablet back to him just as the house lights went down. A Japanese Elvis impersonator stood at the microphone when the lights came back up, and the audience began to cheer and applaud.

Bea nudged Ryan. "Bet that's your dad."

Ryan laughed. "Yeah, we finally found him."

Logan was glad the impersonator stayed true to what Elvis might have worn early on in his career. Japanese Elvis wore a red suit with a pink and red striped shirt and white shoes. He sang Aaron Schroder and Ben Weisman's 1957 hit song, *Got A Lot O' Livin' To Do*, featured on Elvis' *Loving You* LP. Closing his eyes as Japanese Elvis sang, Logan pictured his mom holding the album with its Easter egg blue background, Elvis' face staring pensively at the camera, two slight wrinkles in his brow, his black hair impossibly thick and shiny with product.

Next up was chubby Elvis, a dark-haired man pushing forty, dressed in a brown suit, a pink shirt, and brown loafers. He sang Don Robertson's ditty from 1956, *I'm Counting on You*, mopping his brow as he tried to swivel his hips. The album this song was on was still fresh in Logan's mind as well. It seemed like just yesterday Ramona was sliding that slice of vinyl heaven out of its sleeve, the album cover featuring a black and white photo of Elvis playing guitar, his mouth wide open in song, "Elvis" in pink block letters along the left-hand side of the cover, "Presley" in green across the bottom.

African-American Elvis was up next. Correctly dressed, right down to his blue suede shoes, he shook, rattled, and rolled to the Carl Perkins classic and got a standing ovation from the crowd.

The procession of Elvis impersonators continued, as did the songs. Last up was the only female Elvis impersonator of the night, a gangly woman with a short haircut who chose to sing *First In Line* from the 1956 album *Elvis*. This was yet another album Logan remembered fondly. The cover art was as simple as the album's title, utilizing a photo of Elvis shown in profile, wearing a striped shirt, chin tilted up, singing and playing guitar, the backdrop a firelit gold, his first name in red letters down the left-hand side. Logan thought, when he was younger, Elvis was singing to his first name on the album cover. The artwork made it look as though, if he jumped forward a space, he could take a bite out of the "S."

The female singer was only moderately good. Her voice wasn't low enough, even though the song had been set in a higher key. Afterward, the emcee ran out, removed the microphone from the stand, and went over to the grand piano. "Who wants to sing?"

"He does!" Bea shouted, grabbing Ryan's arm.

"This guy does!" Noah bellowed. He stood up and tried to pull Ryan to his feet.

The emcee squinted at them. "That guy? Well, okay, come on up!"

Ryan ran up the side stairs to the stage, where the emcee sized him up. "Well, you're not dressed like Elvis, but you sure as shit look like him."

The crowd applauded. Ryan, in his blue hoodie and jeans, took a bow.

"What are you going to sing?"

"Just a sec."

Ryan went over to the pianist. "What songs were on *Elvis' Christmas Album*?"

The pianist, a slender man with a soul patch, took a deep breath. "*Blue Christmas, Here Comes Santa Claus, I Believe, I'll Be Home For Christmas, It Is No Secret What God Can Do, O Little Town of Bethlehem, Santa Claus Is Back In Town, Santa Bring My Baby Back To Me, Silent Night, Take My Hand Precious Lord,* and *White Christmas.*"

"Dude, do you know you just rattled those off in alphabetical order?"

"That's how I remember them, kid."

"*O Little Town of Bethlehem* in the key of G."

The pianist nodded and Ryan walked to the center of the stage. The lights dimmed and turned blue. Though Ryan had never heard Elvis sing the song, his rendition sent shivers through Logan, who listened to the song every night before he slept.

"O little town of Bethlehem, how still we see thee lie! Above thy deep and dreamless sleep the silent stars go by. Yet in thy dark streets shineth the everlasting Light. The hopes and fears of all the years are met in thee tonight."

Ryan smiled. He was certain he remembered the song in its entirety from church at Christmastime. "For Christ is born of Mary, and gathered all above. While mortals sleep, the angels keep their watch of wond'ring love. O morning stars, together proclaim the holy birth, And praises sing to God the King, and peace to men on earth!"

He looked out into the audience and was astonished to see not only Bea crying, but other people as well. He kept going. "How silently, how silently, the wondrous Gift is giv'n; So God imparts to human hearts the blessings of His Heav'n. No ear may hear His coming, but in this world of sin, where meek souls will receive Him still, the dear Christ enters in."

Bea wiped her eyes. Noah moved a seat closer and took her hand.

"Where children pure and happy pray to the blessed Child, Where misery cries out to Thee, Son of the mother mild; Where charity stands watching and faith holds wide the door, The dark night wakes, the glory breaks, and Christmas comes once more."

Bea reached out her other hand and took Logan's. The three of them sat there, united in the moment, as Ryan finished the song.

"O holy Child of Bethlehem, descend to us, we pray; Cast out our sin, and enter in, be born in us today. We hear the Christmas angels the great glad tidings tell; oh, come to us, abide with us, our Lord Emmanuel!"

Bar Fifty-Six was silent for a heartbeat before it erupted.

A group seated in back began to chant, "Elvis, Elvis, Elvis!"

Ryan stepped down from the stage and was rushed by friends and strangers. Some reached out to grab him, but he couldn't, for the life of him, figure out why. He thought he had done well, but the sheer force of goodwill surrounding him gave him pause.

37

The kitchen was dark, illuminated only by a slice of light from the Tiffany-style pendant chandelier over the round table in the dining area. Dr. Wendall Johns lifted the plastic magnet shaped like a slice of watermelon off the fridge and took his nephew's note to the table, where he read it thrice and shook his head in disbelief. Logan never went anywhere, but the note was proof that change was in the air.

"At Bar Fifty-Six with new friends. Back soon. Love, L."

It was ten o'clock. His dinner with Nancy had been followed by a stroll through the shops at Caesars Palace. Wendall had been good friends with Nancy's late husband and felt his friend might not be too upset Nancy and he had become close, because things had remained strictly platonic. Nancy worked at Fremont Tech downtown and saved carefully to buy something fabulous once a year to add to either her home or wardrobe. Tonight, she selected a bright khaki, grainy nubuck leather and suede clutch with an ornamental fox head from Burberry that matched one of her favorite cool-weather coats, and Warren picked up a box of pre-embargo Cuban Partagas from Colosseum Cigars, which he like to smoke on his open patio facing the golf course behind his home.

Warren was still at the table, thinking, when the front door opened and he heard a burst of excited chatter. In the foyer, Logan held up his hand so they'd wait. When he found his uncle, he grinned and disappeared, reappearing moments later with the three teenagers in tow. The kid who looked like Elvis spoke first, but Warren barely heard what he said. Counting back seventeen years, to the late eighties, he realized this magnificent young man must be Elvis' and Zella's son, and it took his breath away.

A pretty blond girl who stood between the miraculous young man and a sandy-haired tall kid stepped forward. It was clear to Warren she was repeating a question she'd already asked.

"Yes, yes, I'm Dr. Johns." He rose halfway up from his club chair in greeting and then sank back down. "Please, have a seat." The table seated six, so there was room for all of them if you included the invisible ghost of a legend who died in the summer of seventy-seven.

Noah sat directly across the table from Dr. Johns, with Ryan and one empty seat to his left, and Bea and Logan to his right. "We took Logan to Bar Fifty-Six."

Dr. Johns picked up the note on the table. "Yes."

Logan pulled his tablet from the inside pocket of his jacket and started typing.

The New Elvis

"Thank you for the note on the fridge, Logan. I would have been worried if you hadn't left one. That was considerate." He accepted the tablet. It read: *I had fun.*

Warren typed, *really glad*, and passed it back to him.

Ryan placed his hands flat on the table. Mentally, Warren placed The King's rings on the young man's fingers. He put a treasure Elvis had bought backstage before one of his early concerts on Ryan's ring finger, and the imaginary fourteen-karat gold horseshoe with single-cut diamonds seemed to sparkle in the glow of the light from the stained-glass chandelier. Next, he placed an opulent ring on Ryan's pinkie finger—a crystal opal surrounded by a cluster of diamonds. Elvis' Rising Sun ring went on the young man's other ring finger. It featured a horse head designed after Elvis' beloved Palomino, in fourteen-karat gold, with diamond eyes and a diamond horseshoe around its neck. Ryan was speaking, but Warren didn't hear him. Again, it was Bea's voice that cut through his reverie. "We were saying, we think Ryan's mother came to see you to try and get pregnant."

Warren tried to focus on Bea but was distracted as a perfect dark lock of hair fell squarely down the middle of Ryan's forehead. He had The King's same gorgeous, thick, dark, luxuriant hair made to be styled in a pompadour, the same soft face with prominent cheekbones, the same shape to his brow bone area, the same broad forehead, the same cheeks, the same relatively small mouth, the same full lips, the same left side lip curl, the same broad jaw, the same rounded chin, the same low-riding eyelids, the same startling half-mast blue eyes, the same slightly raised eyebrows, the same broad nose that tapered at the tip.

"You keep looking at him," Bea noted. "Did you know his mother?"

Warren tore his eyes away from Ryan and looked at Bea. "Whose mother?"

"His. Ryan's."

The doctor played dumb. "What's your last name?" He knew Zella had married Eugene Wyatt. She had sent him Christmas cards until the mid-nineties, when they ground to a halt as life took over, the road behind them fading in the rearview mirror.

"Wyatt," Ryan told him, giving the doctor chills. Ryan's voice and inflections were pure Californian, but if you'd raised him in Memphis, he and Elvis would sound as alike as two kernels off the same cob of corn.

Warren stood up and went into the kitchen, where he'd left his new cigars. He snapped on the overhead lights, took the cigar box out of the bag lying on the counter, opened the box, removed a cigar, found a suitable knife among the utensils in the top drawer of a cabinet, and cleanly cut the tip off on the cutting board by the sink.

The teenagers filtered into the kitchen and watched him.

"So you don't remember anyone named Wyatt?" Bea asked.

Noah hiked up his pants. "Maybe she used her maiden name?"

Warren removed the ring wrapper from the cigar, stalling. "What might that be?"

Ryan moved closer. "Her name was Zella Stuart."

Beneath the kitchen's fluorescent lights, Logan saw how much grayer his uncle had gotten, how the salt and pepper years were passing as surely as water erodes stone, how he seemed wearier and more frail.

Warren dug around in the top drawer closest to the sink and pulled out a box of wooden matches. "No. Doesn't sound familiar." He lit his cigar and headed toward the sliding glass door that led to the patio. He turned back. "Excuse me."

Then he stepped outside, sliding the glass door shut behind him.

38

Logan no longer needed Uncle Warren to drop the needle on *Elvis' Christmas Album* for him when he went to bed. He was able to do it himself. Tonight, however, instead of side one, he listened to side two, which kicked off with *O Little Town of Bethlehem*, followed by *Silent Night, There'll Be Peace in the Valley For Me*, and three other songs. He climbed into bed and peeled off his socks by digging the toes of one foot down the back of the sock on the opposite foot, kicking, and repeating. He was cold and unsettled, so he got out of bed and got another comforter from the closet, fanning it out so it landed flat atop his mussed covers. Then he climbed back in, but he was still restless. He got up and went over to his mirror. *What had changed? Why was he feeling so alive?* His face had color and his brown eyes had a brightness to them he'd never seen before. Maybe it was because he went out and had a good time with kids his own age. They had made him feel welcome and accepted and hadn't even given him a hard time when he passed on the beer. But was it just a fluke? And if he ventured out again, would he be treated as he had been tonight or would he be mocked like he was when he was a child?

The clothes he wore were different now. Nancy saw to that. And he was clean, thanks to being able to shower in a tub that wasn't filled with items Ramona had meant to put away. His hair was cut every month at a barbershop on Winchester, and his fingernails were short and clean. He had even learned to shave the sparse facial hair that was beginning to appear.

Barefoot, he crept downstairs. The light in the dining area had been turned off, but the stove light was on in the kitchen. Logan peered around the corner, into the living room. He watched as Uncle Wendall buried a folder filled with paperwork beneath old newspapers, catalogs, and junk mail in a bin next to the fireplace. The receptacle held flammables used to get logs blazing when they wanted a nice fire. Whatever Uncle Wendall hid in the bin was meant to burn.

Logan snuck back upstairs just as *Silent Night* was ending, and by the time *It's No Secret What God Can Do* was coming to an end, he realized Uncle Wendall was standing in his open doorway. The room was dark, but Logan pretended to be asleep. Side two had come to an end. The needle lifted up and returned to the beginning of the side for a replay. At some point during the night, when Logan was younger, Uncle Wendall would come in, lift the needle, and turn the stereo off. But he didn't do it now. Instead, he stood and listened to *O Little Town of Bethlehem*. Midway through the song, he left the doorway and headed down the hallway.

Logan heard his uncle's bedroom door shut. He waited through *Silent Night* and *There'll Be Peace in the Valley* before he dared to get up. Then he went downstairs, poked around in the fireplace bin till he found the folder, and looked inside.

He was looking at the medical records for Ryan's mother.

Scanning them, he found what he was looking for on a slip of blue paper tucked toward the back of the stack of pages. It read, "Elvis Presley, T-8A-14226, 8/19/74."

39

With his success in Vegas, Ryan and Noah went to karaoke contests held at bars throughout Los Angeles generally on school nights, but Ryan tried to perform early and get back home by his ten o'clock curfew, and the Wyatts were none the wiser. In addition to singing in public, the trip to Vegas had thrown fuel on Ryan's urge to find his biological father. Most afternoons, he found himself in Bea's bedroom, where they surfed websites and forums. One Tuesday not long after their trip, Ryan practiced hip swivels in the mirror while Bea read recent messages on FindUrBiologicalFather.net, SpermDaddy.com, and DonorSiblingsUnite.com. Ryan had posted his picture and information on the sites, hoping someone who had donated sperm in Vegas prior to 1988 would contact him.

"*I connected with my real dad this past weekend,*" Bea read aloud, "*and he was everything I dreamed he would be and more. He said he didn't want a family because he travels for work so much and is never in one place for long, but now that he's met me, he plans to keep in touch.*"

Ryan stopped swiveling. "Wow."

"Yeah. And Mary Eisenhart from Missouri is still ranting about the fact that sperm banks protect donor confidentiality, but no one considers how that affects kids."

Ryan came over and jumped on the bed.

Bea shoved the laptop at him. "Here. You read."

She got up, went to her drawer of meds, took out a few vials, popped the caps, threw a few tablets into her mouth, drank some water, and returned the vials to the drawer.

Ryan read her a story posted by a woman with the handle "Dubby905."

"*When my husband couldn't get me pregnant, I went to a sperm bank. I never told my husband our daughter isn't his. When we wanted a second child, I used the same donor so my children would be related. I will never tell my family what I did, and I'm not sorry. How could I be, when I have such a wonderful life with two beautiful kids and a husband who loves me?*"

Bea flopped down on the bed. "Aw!"

Ryan opened another window on the screen. "I wanted to show you this one."

A picture of a blond woman in her early twenties appeared beside her message.

"*If you really want to find out who your dad is, find the donor card. My mom kept a medical card from New Jersey Cryogenics in her recipe box. I found it one day when I was looking for a brownie recipe. Yes, brownies—wink! Anyway, I asked my mom about it. She told me a long time ago that I was conceived via artificial insemination, so it was no big deal. She kept the card because she thought we might need it for medical reasons, in case I got sick and we had to check out the donor's medical history. So, the card had a donor number on it, which was my dad's number. If you can find your card and get your dad's number, you will be a lot closer to figuring out who he is (if you want to). Me, I don't care too much. Just thought I'd share this as another way to find out who your dad is (if you want to know).*"

Bea slumped back into the pillows. Her words were beginning to slur. "Did you find your donor card?"

"No, but I'll keep looking. If I was able to find Dr. Johns' card, maybe she kept a donor card too."

Bea closed her eyes. "Fat lot of help Dr. Johns was."

Ryan read another entry, this one by a young man calling himself BaySurfer.

"*I've been searching for my biological father for six years. My parents don't care about me and never did. They never told me I was a sperm donor baby, and it's probably good they didn't. I would have left home years ago. As it is, I have lost years I could have been searching for him, and I will never forgive them for lying to me my whole life.*"

Another entry, this one by a woman just offering her first name, Megan, read, "*I just found out my dad isn't my dad, and I am pissed. I am an only child and always wanted brothers and sisters. What if I have half-brothers and half-sisters out there who are looking for me? How do I find them?*"

Then there was an anonymous note from a sperm donor posted in a forum titled, "From Us Dads to You." "*I know some of you are asking yourselves, is my dad thinking about me, wherever he is? The answer is a resounding YES. Sure, some guys are donors in college or whatever, and they move on and they have lives and they do seem to forget. But if they were really honest with themselves, they would have to admit that once in a while, even if it is very infrequently, they do wonder if they have any kids out there they don't know about, and if they do, where they are and how they might be doing. Do they look like me? Do they have any similar traits? Do they have similar interests? Do they have similar talents? There will always be a yearning to know.*"

Ryan looked over at Bea. She had fallen asleep with her mouth open. He read one last post, this one by a sad-looking woman who went by the handle "FindYou15."

"*I have wanted to find my biological dad for years, but my mom won't let me. She is afraid of losing me. We don't have much money, and unless I get a scholarship, I won't be going to college. How does she know my dad wouldn't be able to help me? Help us? She has been a single mom all these years to my sister and I, and I am ready to give up. I have spent my whole life fantasizing about the father I don't know. Does this happen to boys who don't know their fathers too?*"

A tear leaked from corner of Ryan's eye. He brushed it away, covered Bea with a peach-colored throw blanket, unplugged the laptop, and went home.

40

Just as Don Draper and his friends pulled together their own agency from the spoils of Sterling Cooper, twelve years into the new millennium, Nicole "Marilyn" Coffey left the cutthroat environs of *Flash* to start her own tabloid in the last rent-controlled apartment complex in the Valentino Heights section of the Hollywood Hills.

The show of solidarity began the week Marilyn blasted a hole through the back of her bedroom closet, old England countryside style, so she could connect her unit through the back of Tobias Vada's bedroom closet into his one-bedroom unit and then forge a hole through the back of Tobias' living room closet in through the back of Pia Sutherland's living room closet, creating one giant living space shared by friends. The three had been lucky enough to rent apartments in The Argyle Arms, a strangely named complex that had been rent controlled since the seventies. When next-door neighbor Ira Jarvis died in 1986, Tobias, who had been living in the complex since 1982, convinced the on-site landlords, Bob and Ethel Hector, to rent the unit to Pia, who had just moved to Hollywood from San Francisco. Then, in 1998, when neighbor Hugh Braxton was ready to give up his one-bedroom to move into his boyfriend's two-bedroom condo in West Hollywood, Tobias asked Marilyn, who had just moved to Hollywood from Vegas, to take Braxton's pad.

The three had worked together at *Flash*—Tobias since 1983, Pia since 1986, and Marilyn since 1998—but of the three of them, Marilyn had had the roughest go. When she walked into the offices at *Flash* on Hollywood Boulevard thirteen years earlier, she had been the tender age of twenty, having left home in Milwaukee at eighteen, heading to Vegas, where she spent two years as a Monroe look-alike in the *Legends Live Tribute* at the Kalahari Hotel & Casino on South Las Vegas Boulevard.

Nicole was Marilyn incarnate, from the platinum blonde hair, pert nose, full mouth, and curvaceous figure, right down to the little-girl voice. Her nails were always immaculate and polished with Chanel Le Vernis in a constantly changing palette—her favorite shade being number 209 Marilyn, a hot pink Monroe would have loved. *Flash* sent their Marilyn, whom they never called Nicole, on jobs that compromised her sexually and, after two years of this, Alastair Neville, owner of *Flash,* flew in from London expressly to see her. Her assignment was to spend the weekend with him in his deluxe suite at the Mondrian, theoretically taking notes on the redesign of L.A. Bureau Chief Cecil Bertrand's office. That had been the final straw.

Tobias dropped onto Marilyn's white sofa and kicked off his flip-flops before he put his feet up on the cushions. Everything about him was long, from his face to his arms to his legs to his hair, which he tied back in a thick brown, gray-streaked ponytail. He had a doctorate from Columbia in political science and a quick mind. How he'd ended up writing for the tabloids had nothing to do with his intelligence and everything to do with his joblessness at the time *Flash* offered him a cool grand a week to chase down pregnant starlets and drug-addled producers.

Pia lifted Tobias' feet, plunked herself down on the sofa, and repositioned his feet on her lap. At six feet tall, she drew attention wherever she went, and she accented her height by wearing heels from her extensive collection of Miu Miu, Prada, and Casadei designer pumps. Her dark blonde hair had been frosted since the early eighties, and she never missed her monthly touch-up with her hairdresser, Dmitry, a one-name wonder in the world of styling tresses who ran a salon in Toluca Lake. Like Tobias, she was well educated, having earned a master's degree in psychology from Stanford. When *Flash* ran an ad in *The Los Angeles Times* looking for new reporters "with varied backgrounds," she applied and was offered the job. A thousand bucks a week seemed too good to be true. That was before she found herself on her knees, working for Daily Maids, cleaning stars' homes while combing through their personal items.

Tobias sat up. "Cecil told Genevieve you're barred from the office, and he had Reuben go through your computer. Did you leave anything incriminating behind?"

Marilyn smiled slyly and left the room. They heard the bathroom door shut, and a few minutes later, the toilet was flushed.

She came back. "I'm sorry, what were you asking me?"

"Anything on your computer?" Tobias was sitting up now, his bare feet flat on the hardwood floor.

"Just a budget I worked out to start my own tabloid, who I would steal from *Flash* to come work with me, and how much we could pay ourselves after expenses."

"If you start a rival tabloid, won't you be in breach of contract?" Tobias wondered.

"Never signed anything. They were so anxious to hire me, they skipped that."

Tobias frowned. "They're going to hack you."

"Bring it. We've got to get Logan on board. I've already spoken to Bob and Ethel about extra space. Next to the laundry, there's a studio with a bathroom he can use, and I've already ordered the computers and software he'll need."

The Logan in question was Logan Lockhart. After he earned his GED, he went to Fremont Tech, where Nancy worked, and graduated with a bachelor's in graphic arts. Not long after that, *Flash* came calling, and he quickly became the graphics master who gave the weekly its eye-catching style. Even though he didn't speak, everyone loved him. They knew that feeling close to his colleagues was essential to Logan's happiness and, moreover, if he were to someday get his voice back, he'd love to become a reporter himself.

Tobias wore a pensive expression. "They'll set you up as the perfect example of why someone shouldn't leave."

Marilyn ignored him. "What do you think about sealed stories with perforated sides, so that once you open them, you get a card stock photo and story printed alongside it? And on the outside, we'll pose a tantalizing question alongside our logo, like, *Who's Been Spotted Whitewater Rafting Naked?* You'd buy the issue and tear off the front to find a glossy photo of a guy like Scott

Wardlaw whitewater rafting in the nude, along with the story. And I've already thought of the perfect name for our new tabloid: *Daily Celebrity*. What do you guys think?"

41

Ryan could still manage to sidestep his father, since his father was avoiding him, but by the time high school graduation rolled around, he knew he had to make amends with his mother. He had been accepted at USC and was intent on studying performing arts education with the dream of someday being in charge of the annual musicals at some tiny private school in New Hampshire. He didn't know why New Hampshire, but it seemed about as far away from California as he could get. But, to be at peace, he also needed to continue his search for his birth dad. And then there was the matter of Bea. She wasn't getting any better, and he didn't want to be stuck in a downtown Los Angeles dorm, wondering how she was every day. To commute was out of the question. Eleven miles east, the school might take only twenty minutes or and exhausting two hours to get to on the I-10, depending on the traffic, and then another twenty or two coming back from classes.

The Monday after graduation, Ryan found his mother in the dining room, sorting and polishing silver. He watched as she spread it out on the dining room table, placing it in piles on different hand towels. She started on one group, dipping her cloth into the silver polish and rubbing each piece until it gleamed. These days, she looked older, more careworn, but as beautiful as ever. New laugh lines had formed near her mouth and eyes. If her hair was going gray, she hid it with dye.

Ryan spoke first. "You got a minute?"

She looked up at him, broke into a smile, and her face was transformed from beautiful to radiant. Ever since Ryan found out he wasn't Gene's son, he had given her the brush-off any time she wanted to talk, which had hurt him as much as it hurt her. He had ignored Bea after he'd seen her with Kincaid, and he knew how much damage ignoring someone you loved caused. He sat down at the table.

"Do you need any help?"

She shook her head. "What do you want to talk about?"

He was overwhelmed with relief. "Anything. Everything. Tell me about meeting dad. What were you like back then? What was going on?"

She kept on polishing the silver. "The prequel too?"

He nodded, ready to listen. She told him she'd been engaged to a man before she'd met Gene. He'd been on his way to see her when he boarded a plane in Michigan that never made it past a grove of trees outside Detroit before it crashed. He'd been one of many fatalities. They'd been inseparable, like Ryan and Bea, and always knew they'd be together. "I was set on becoming the young Mrs. Enright. He gave me a promise ring our senior year. I'd never dated anyone else and never wanted to. We even discussed how many children we'd have."

Ryan identified with that. His romance with Bea was unquestioned.

"I was going to become the most famous female magician in Vegas—no small feat, considering the field is dominated by men—and he was going to have his own shop where he could do what he loved."

Ryan picked up a spoon she'd polished and studied his distorted reflection.

"Which was?"

"Oh, he was in love with cars. Second to me, of course, but he did love cars and had an uncanny knack of diagnosing whatever ailed them. I can't even count how many times he stopped to help someone when we were headed out on a date!" Her mind was far away as she recalled the past, and Ryan sat in silence, watching as she picked up a ladle and examined it. "We spoke the night before his flight. We were going to find an apartment for him. The next day, I got a call from his father."

Ryan reached out his hand and she held it for a moment before she resumed polishing. "It's okay. It's long healed. When I think of him now, it's all good, happy memories."

"So what happened?"

"I was grieving. When they talk about an aching heart, they mean it literally. By the time the holidays rolled around, I had the notion to go see a fertility specialist I'd heard about from a waitress at The Flamingo. His office was off Las Vegas Boulevard, set back from the road on a little street called Harmon, squeezed in between two larger buildings. The cheerfulness of the Christmas lights and decorations gave me hope. I wanted a baby because I needed someone to love."

"What about a dog or a new boyfriend?"

Zella laughed. "Tried a cat *and* a dog *and* a roommate, and had basically sworn off men. Mothers talk about the unconditional love they have for their children. I had that with Glenn. Even with him gone—especially with him gone—I felt a deep need for that again."

Ryan wanted her to know he knew more than she might think. "So, you went to Las Vegas Fertility Associates to see Dr. Wendall Johns."

Zella didn't seem surprised he knew the name of both her doctor and the clinic. She knew Ryan had overheard his dad and grandparents talking and was aware he'd found the business card clipped inside her old calendar.

"He had a Christmas tree with ornaments made of clay impressions of handprints, with names and years of births. Each print was impossibly small, no larger than a plum, and perfect. I knew as soon as I saw that tree, I wanted him to hang an ornament for you as soon as you were born. I had money from Glenn's family, so I could afford artificial insemination. I decided to let the doctor select the father, and he did."

"And he never told you who it was?"

Zella put more polish on the cloth. "One can only imagine. I met your father not long after I'd become successfully impregnated with the donor sperm. Oh, your dad was so handsome back then. He had just a touch of gray in his hair, and he was thinner, less stressed. I don't know if things will get better or worse when he retires. I really don't think he should, entirely. He's so driven."

"Tell me about it."

Zella put some of the clean silver back into the velvet-lined case that stood open on the table, its hinges yawning wide. "So, we fell in love and got married and you were born, end of story."

"Don't you ever wonder who he was?" Ryan asked.

"Who?"

"My real father. You must have some idea."

Zella closed the lid on the silver case. "Dr. Johns keeps those matters confidential. If you've met him, you already know that."

42

Tobias Vada had a lunch interview that day with Helen Hester at a new restaurant called The Topiary on Beverly Boulevard, but first, he wanted to stop by *Flash* and convince Logan to jump ship and join his friends at the new *Daily Celebrity*.

He was forced to turn in his parking pass when he quit to go work with Marilyn, so he parked his black Fiat Croma on Sunset, across from the garage entrance, and waited until Cecil

Bertrand peeled out, the tires on his Mercedes squealing, heading east, destination unknown. There was a fire door in back of the building that remained unlocked and led to a stairwell that served every level and led to the roof. With long strides, Tobias took the steps three at a time, ascending to the eighth floor, where he poked his head out into the hallway and approached the front desk, where the receptionist, Genevieve Krantz usually sat, combing through rival tabloids, marking stories *Flash* should follow up on. As luck would have it, she was away from her desk, so Tobias snuck down the hall and poked his head into Logan's office, making sure Logan knew he'd arrived by walking around the partition and tipping the brim of his houndstooth driver's cap, knowing the movement would catch his eye.

Logan had selective mutism, and while few had asked him about it, Tobias and his colleagues discussed his disorder endlessly. While most cases of SM allowed sufferers to speak in certain situations or to a privileged few, Logan's case was so severe he never said a word. His condition co-existed with persistent anxiety and social shyness to the point where he often stopped working when someone came into his office because he could no longer focus on what he was doing. To communicate, he had upgraded from his old tablet to an iPad, opened to the Notes Plus application. He reached beyond his pen mug for it now, typed a message, and passed it across the desk to Tobias.

How did you get in?

Tobias laughed and typed his reply. *Waited for Bertrand to leave.*

Logan responded, *Let's go down to the courtyard. It's not safe here.*

Tobias raised his eyebrows.

After locking his office door, Logan led Tobias to the elevators across from the receptionist's desk. Genevieve had returned to her post, and her jaw went slack when she saw Tobias, who smiled and nodded politely. Something about hanging with Logan reminded Tobias that talking was incredibly overrated.

As they descended to the ground floor, they stood beside each other, unable to avoid glancing at the mirrored elevator walls facing them on three sides. Tobias looked like a stretched-out, pale Gumby with a long ponytail, pushing fifty and tired. Logan, half his age and half a foot shorter, looked like a prep school kid in a lavender Izod shirt, his chestnut hair carefully styled into a spiky fauxhawk rising to a peak three inches from the top of his head. Even their footwear was drastically different. Tobias wore sandals, showing off his bare feet, while Logan wore canvas high-tops laced past his ankles, beneath the cuffs of his skinny jeans.

They walked through the lobby and went out the massive glass doors, into the courtyard where plastic tables and chairs were arranged in groups around stainless steel trashcans fitted with metal ashtray lids, and took seats at a table in the center of the open space, where the scalding sunshine felt as merciless as a four-hundred-degree oven.

Tobias stripped off his jacket while Logan typed a message, passing him the iPad when he was done. In order to read the screen, it was necessary to hunch over, creating a shadow to block direct sunlight from bleaching the words on the screen.

How are you?
Tobias smiled and typed his response. *I'm good. And you?*
Need to get out of here. The place went nuts after you all left.
That's why I'm here. We want you and Dan to join us.
I thought you didn't ask because you didn't want us.
Don't be silly. Dan is an asshole, but he's great reporter.
And me?
The best graphics guy ever.
Great. Let me go clean out my desk.
Aren't you going to ask about money?
No. I would pay you guys to get me out of here right about now.

Then I won't bother telling you you'll be getting three grand a week.

Logan broke into a wide grin. *Twice what I'm making now. Don't tell Marilyn that.*

I won't.

When they got back upstairs, a security guard was waiting by the eighth floor elevator doors. He was as buff as club bouncer, dressed in a dark blue uniform. "Tobias Vada?"

As Logan exited the elevator, Tobias shrank back and pressed the down button on the wall panel. "Just leaving," he said.

"Mind if I escort you?" The guard stepped into the elevator with him and the doors closed.

At her desk, Genevieve looked guilty. "I had to call Cecil. Tobi doesn't work here anymore."

Logan scowled at her, went to his office, unlocked his door, and headed to his desk. After scooping his spare sweater into his backpack, he sat down at his desk and copied his hard drive. He pocketed the thumb drives, pushed his desk chair in, grabbed his iPad and backpack, and headed out, leaving his office unlocked.

He went to Genevieve's desk and placed his backpack near her in-box so his hands were free. After typing a message, he handed her the iPad.

Genevieve read it, a quizzical expression on her face. *Going out for a late lunch.*

Logan always ate at his desk, brown bagging it religiously.

Okay, she typed, handing the iPad back.

To keep his word, Logan had a bowl of soup in the cafeteria on the fourth floor. Then he left the office building, without looking back.

Tobias was maneuvering out of his tight parking space on Sunset when he saw Logan exit the *Flash* office building and trot down the steps to the street. Tobias lowered the driver's side window, stuck out an arm, and caught his eye. Grinning as he dodged a truck, Logan navigated through traffic and made it to the sidewalk.

Tobias lowered the window on the passenger side. "Where's your Caddy?"

Logan shook his head. He had sold his graduation gift—a yellow '54 Cadillac convertible just like the King's—for a very important cause: ascertaining paternity for Ryan that he was indeed Elvis' biological son.

"You don't have it anymore?" Tobias was incredulous. "How are you getting around?"

Logan pointed at a bus as it passed, and Tobias' eyes followed it.

"Jeez," Tobias muttered. "Get in."

Tobias unlocked the passenger side and Logan hopped in.

"You quit, right?"

Logan nodded.

"Great. Well, join me for lunch. We're meeting a very classy TV star. You know who Helen Hester is?"

43

In the end, Ryan was glad he'd had a heart-to-heart with his mom because she helped him decide to take a year off before college and offered to pay for Bea's eighteenth birthday gift on June twenty-ninth—a trip for two to Memphis so they could tour Graceland. She didn't ask Ryan why he wanted to tour Elvis' home. He suspected she knew he was curious as to why he looked so much like the King and wondered if it had anything to do with his father possibly being an Elvis impersonator. He was sure if it had crossed his mind, it had crossed hers, but they didn't go there. They stopped at the threshold of agreeing his father's identity was a secret kept by Dr. Johns.

The New Elvis

Both newly graduated from high school, Bea and Ryan checked into the Presley's Heartbreak Hotel in Memphis the last Friday in June, sans chaperones, with both the Edwins' and his parents' blessings. Ryan thought it was mostly because Bea was so sick that they weren't being strict with them. At that point, Mrs. Edwin swore Ryan was the only person who could make her happy.

The room they checked into on Elvis Presley Boulevard was kind of shabby, with blue and gold diamond-patterned bedspreads on matching king-sized beds. Ryan's mom arranged the trip so, for all appearances, they slept separately even if they shared the room. The only touch of Elvis in the two-hundred-square-feet of their own private heaven were black and white framed photos of him over each bed, one from his early years and one taken toward the end of his career.

Bea took her meds and fell asleep before she'd even unpacked, so Ryan watched the endless stream of Elvis movies on TV, hoping she'd wake up so they could take the shuttle to Beale Street and grab some grub. The flight had worn her out. She slept on her stomach with both arms thrown over her head and wrapped around a pillow, her head turned toward him so he could see her pale face partially covered by a tumble of golden curls. It was hard for him to decide which one to watch—Elvis in *Blue Hawaii* or his very own angel in dreamland.

By the time midnight rolled around, he was restless. He had never been to Memphis before and might never return, so he didn't want to lose out. He rose and muted the TV, leaving it on so the room wouldn't be completely dark when she woke up. Throughout the room, the screen emitted an otherworldly bluish-green glow.

The night was humid and the air, heavy as wet laundry, weighed on him as he made his way through the lobby. He saw the shuttle out front, so he made a last-minute dash to see if they were heading to Beale. They were, with a return bus at two in the morning. Just enough time to catch a bite, grab a meal in a container for Bea, and make it back.

When the shuttle stopped at the Hard Rock Café, the charm of its brick façade, green awnings, and white latticework rails caught his eye. On impulse, he sprang off the shuttle, made his way to the brass double-door entrance, and swung the right-hand door wide. It was crowded inside and no one seemed to notice him at first, but by the time he had his menu, made his selections, and was staring at the rock memorabilia covering the walls, more and more heads were turning his way. He smiled at everyone who stared at him, and they quickly looked away, whispering to themselves.

The waiter who came to refill his water glass bent down beside him and spoke in a low voice Ryan could barely hear above the restaurant chatter. "You do an Elvis show, right? You're, like, one of those tribute guys?"

"No. Just graduated high school and I haven't decided what I'm going to do yet."

"I feel like I took a trip in the Wayback Machine."

Ryan gave him a blank stare.

Incredulous, the waiter shook his head in disbelief. "The *Rocky and Bullwinkle* cartoons? Your parents are probably old enough to remember them. Sherman and Mr. Peabody used the Wayback to time travel and change history. It was pretty rad."

Change history, Ryan thought. *Yeah, I'd go back and grab a seat in the clinic where my mom met Dr. Johns and listen in. Then I'd search his files and find out who I am.*

The waiter was still chattering away. "There are music execs here tonight, man. One of them is my brother-in-law. Can you sing?"

Ryan shrugged. "Some people seem to think so."

Condensation trickled down the side of the waiter's water pitcher and dripped off.

"Shit, man, people only say that when they're *really* good. You're missing the accent, though. You gotta try to talk like him."

"I do?"

The waiter suddenly realized he needed to be working instead of standing around.

"Your food should be up shortly," he said, turning on his heel, heading to another table.

Ryan looked around at the inquisitive faces. He felt like a new exhibit at the J. Paul Getty Museum. This never happened in Los Angeles, where you'd run into B-list stars at the local gym. There were so many beautiful people in Southern California who looked like someone famous and barely drew a second glance that being in Memphis made him feel like a bug in a jar. Strangely enough, he didn't mind.

44

Marilyn set Logan up in his own apartment off the laundry room, and now that they were greenlighted for production, his days and nights were spent, with intermittent catnaps, laying out each issue. Today, however, was special. They were off to the hospital to visit Belle Gilbert, a tomboyish reporter who often teamed up on jobs with Graham Harvey, a portly Brit who looked like the mascot for Bob's Big Boy.

When Marilyn and Logan arrived with the cake, Pia was tying bits of curled ribbon into Belle's raven topknot and Tobias was arranging a hot pink spread over Belle's thin cotton blanket. A sign reading, "You're 38 and You Look Great," was taped over the bed; it covered a painting by an unknown artist of a man herding sheep across a field. It was Belle's birthday, and friends were invited to show up anytime between two and four, when Highland Hospital and Medical Center staffers seemed to honor an afternoon siesta. Marilyn was in designer duds, and Logan had donned his only suit, which was outdated and in need of a pressing. While Logan held out a box no larger than a cigarette lighter, Marilyn went over to the bedside table and set the cake down.

Restless, Belle untangled her gangly legs from her covers and reached out for Logan. He blushed furiously, hugged her, and handed her the box. She unwrapped it without taking her eyes off his smiling face. It was a silver charm of a pad of paper with a pencil resting atop it. She held it up for all to see.

"You have a charm bracelet?" Tobias asked.

"Sure," Graham said. "I've seen her wear it."

"It's Monet," Pia added, "and this will make her thirteenth charm."

Tobias shook his head. "You guys don't miss anything. What's up, Logan? You couldn't have found an appendix charm?"

Belle giggled. "Right? Who gets their appendix out when they're thirty-eight? Oops, I mean thirty-two." She glanced over her shoulder. "That sign is wrong. Anyway, thank you, Logan."

Logan stared down at his only pair of dress shoes but kept a smile on his face.

Marilyn tossed a sample copy of the first issue of *DC* to Graham just as Kevin "Kevlar" Larson walked in, spotted the tabloid, ran over to Graham, and snatched it. Logan stepped back. He hadn't gotten to know Kevlar as well as the others had, but he knew him by reputation. The reporter had earned his nickname because he'd successfully dodged gunfire in the midst of a bank heist in Palm Springs in 2002 to get an exclusive. The robbers were so impressed by his ballsiness, they told him their life stories, hoping he would make them famous. The Feebs already knew who the robbers were. The crooks had knocked off three banks in the area within four months but had managed to hide between scores better than rattlers in weeds. After Kevlar put the cap back on his pen and moved away from the robbers to put his tape recorder back in his bag, sharpshooters had the thieves in their crosshairs and dropped them cold with headshots no more than ten seconds after Kevlar pressed the off button on his Sony.

"Hey!" Graham protested.

Pia brought him a piece of cake and a plastic fork. "Here, have this."

Graham accepted the plate and smiled. "No one approach me. This is mine."

"That's only a sample issue," Marilyn told everyone.

Earlier that day, she had taken the 101-South six short miles to Perfect Perforation Printers, an aluminum-sided single-story building with an expansive parking lot, where she met Chester Mowbrey and followed him to an office that looked like a cabin room in Oregon, decked out with mounted hunting trophies, despite the fact Mowbrey looked like someone you'd sooner find in a seedy bar than the woods. Short and swarthy, the top buttons of his dress shirt were undone so he could display his hirsute chest. While he was quick to say he wouldn't do her printing job, he nevertheless hoisted a stack of one hundred sample copies onto his desk and pushed the bundle toward her. "Clay Dayton's Wife at Death's Door," by Kevin Larson, in Poynter Agate font, begged readers to rip open the seal and read the inside piece. She tore off the top and examined the photo of Caroline next to Kevlar's story. It looked good.

Mowbrey gave Marilyn the name and number of a printer in San Francisco, but she persisted. "Are you sure you can't do the work?"

Mowbrey all but pushed her into the hallway.

"It's Cecil, isn't it?"

Mowbrey allowed his eyes to travel the length of her body. "I can see why Neville enjoyed your company. Can you do a little laugh like Monroe, sweet and sexy?"

Marilyn's voice was cold. "Thank you for the referral."

The fact that Mowbrey wouldn't run the first issue was even more bothersome in light of the fact that the Dayton scoop was an exclusive. Logan knew the story from having done the layout and could picture the scene as clearly as if he'd been there.

After country singer Clay Dayton's wife Caroline had given birth to Clay Junior, Kevlar stomped around outside Santa Del Rey Hospital, crushed a smoked cigarette under the heel of his cowboy boot, and squinted in the bright sunlight as he talked on his cell phone. "I'm going back in. Maybe the grandparents will show."

Marilyn agreed. "It's their first, so I wouldn't be surprised. What's your cover for getting close enough to get a picture of the newborn?"

"Don't have one."

"Yeah, what good is a cover, anyway?" Marilyn knew Kev was clever enough to come up with a way to get the exclusive without her input, so she'd let him do his thing.

Logan knew this birth was important but almost insignificant when compared to Lisa Marie Presley's visit to St. John's Hospital in Santa Monica to deliver Danielle in May of '89, when a reporter talked a parking attendant into showing him an entrance doctors used to get into the hospital. Lisa Maria was supposedly on the third floor. Heading there, the reporter found the entire wing reserved for the mother and her newborn. Rounding a corner, he found himself face to face with four security guards who accosted him, then tailed him out of the parking garage. Reporters had assumed all guises in an attempt to reach Lisa Maria's room, including that of patient, doctor, nurse, and priest, but none of their efforts were successful. A freelancer working for *The National Enquirer* had been hired as a security guard working the graveyard shift, and he had the best chance of anyone to get the shot worth a million dollars in worldwide sales. His method was ingenious. Alone with the baby in the nursery, he unscrewed a fluorescent bulb so that it flickered, and then he popped off two shots. When a nurse saw the flashes and accused him of taking photos, he pointed to the flickering light and claimed it had caused the flashes she'd seen. Later, on a restroom break, he went down to the parking garage and dropped the film in the trash for his cohort, who was scheduled to pick it up. Hours later, the lab developed two photos of Elvis' first grandchild.

Logan knew Kevlar didn't need to go that far, but he pictured him as he entered the maternity wing. With paparazzi tailing him, new father Clay Dayton had left the hospital, likely to return later with his or his wife's parents. After he departed, the glut of reporters anxious to get a statement from hospital officials dissipated.

No one knew a bigger story was about to unfold. After new mother Caroline Dayton was wheeled into her private room, she had difficulty breathing. Frantic, she searched for her call button, to no avail. Kevlar was outside her door and, with no medical personnel nearby, he ran to her side. Reaching out for Kev with one hand while clutching the bed railing with the other, Caroline caught his sleeve and tried to say something before she lost consciousness. Kev listened to the distant chatter down the hallway, and a split second later, he sprang into action. He found the call button beneath the bedding and pressed it.

A nurse rushed in. "What happened?"

Not waiting for an answer, she pushed Kev aside, blocking Caroline from his sight as she bent over the bed. Kev pulled out his camera and readied for a shot just as the nurse leapt back, hit the code blue emergency button to alert specialists trained to resuscitate dying patients, and flew out of the room to find Caroline's doctor.

Kev walked over to the bed and framed his first shot with his compact digital Olympus. Facial cyanosis had set in, turning Caroline's complexion a bruised indigo. Click, click, click, and click. Kev took shots from the left and right sides of the bed, as well as from the foot and from above, raising himself up so he could shoot downward.

Caroline's doctor rushed in just as Kev moved away from the bed. Barely giving Kev a second glance, Dr. Vipont jumped on the bed and straddled Caroline to administer CPR. The nurse returned with an ambu bag and administered mouth to mouth with the reservoir of oxygen to force ventilation while the doctor continued chest compressions.

Kev had the pictures he wanted, but he remained in the corner of the room, his palms sweaty and his pulse pounding. The new mother was flatlining. He knew the statistics: only five to ten percent of those who received CPR survived, and if they didn't get her heart started soon, brain death was imminent. The code blue team flooded the room. Caroline was given medications to stimulate her heart while Vipont continued chest compressions. The flat-line tone on the monitor sputtered and changed. Kev looked at his watch. The new mother had been gone four and a half minutes.

Vipont climbed off the woman and stepped back. "Get her to the ICU."

Now alone with the doctor, Kev stuck his hand in his pocket and pressed the record button on his Sony. "Thank you for saving her life."

Vipont turned. "Mr. Dayton?"

Kev wagered this doctor didn't like country music and wouldn't recognize Clay, and he'd been right. "Do you know what happened?"

She took off one of her surgical gloves and shook his hand. "Last time I saw something nearly identical to this was five years ago with a schoolteacher who also had a c-section. She had an amniotic fluid embolism."

Kev's puzzlement showed on his face.

"It's a complication of childbirth. Amniotic fluid enters the bloodstream and passes through the lungs, causing cardiac arrest. Embolisms of this sort are very rare."

"When can I see her?"

"Stay put. We'll come get you when she's stable."

Now, still in a hospital room, but at Highland instead of Santa Del Rey, all eyes were on Kevlar as he read his story to the group.

"Issue number one, folks, all mine! Just as I predicted!"

Pia cut more slices of cake. "Yeah, Kev, it's all about you. Who's not here yet?"

"Us." Dan Quaid and his cousin Ron Fletcher stood in the doorway.

Marilyn crossed the room. "You must be Dan's cousin."

He shook her hand. "Ron Fletcher, formerly of *The Pulse* in Chicago."

"I've got to talk to you," Dan told Marilyn. "But first, everyone, yes, this is Ron. He was writing for *The Pulse*, but I convinced him he'd be better off out here with me."

There was no doubt in Marilyn's mind that Dan and Ron were family. Both he and his cousin looked like ferrets, with sharp noses, pointy incisors, and dark hair slicked back with gel. Dan said his looks, or lack thereof, helped him get stories. Few celebrities expected a homely guy to be a threat. Pia gave Marilyn a silent signal to come and talk while Dan and Ron studied the sample issue of *DC*.

"What's up?"

Pia handed Marilyn the knife. "I recognize Fletcher. He was at *Flash*, talking to Bertrand a week before you left."

"Maybe he wanted to join Dan at *Flash* before they knew I'd be starting my own tabloid. Dan said he wanted Ron to move out here."

"I'm not so sure. What if Fletcher is a friend of Cecil's and he's here to spy on us? In fact, what if Dan and he are *both* spying on us?"

Marilyn knew Pia didn't like Dan, so by default, she wouldn't like his cousin. Pia was suspicious of how Dan got sensational stories she never managed to score, and Marilyn wrote it off to professional jealousy.

Pia was insistent. "Something fishy is going on."

Dan walked up behind them and Pia jumped. "What are you girls whispering about over here, and what do I have to do to get a piece of cake?"

Belle finished unwrapping gifts from Dan and his cousin. Each box held a medium-sized cashmere sweater—a solid blue one from Dan and an argyle print in olive, white, and gold from Ron.

"So, we've got a problem," Marilyn announced. "PPP refused to do a full print run, but Chester Mowbrey gave me a contact in San Francisco."

Ron stepped forward. "I know I'm the new guy, but my old college roommate's dad owns a press in Chicago. Have you heard of Insert Press and Distribution?"

Marilyn's jaw dropped and the ferret cousins chuckled.

45

Before Ryan could take a bite into his Hard Rock legendary ten-ounce burger, a tiny humpbacked man who looked past ninety made his way across the restaurant and stood before him.

"Pardon me for interrupting," he said, "but I knew Elvis back in the day, and you're his spitting image."

Ryan pushed his chair back and rose up in greeting. "Have a seat."

The man pulled out a chair and settled into it. He had a smallish head, a beaklike nose, and coffee-bean-colored eyes that looked alert and curious. What hair remained on his head was gauzy grey. "Last thing I worked on was his *Live on Stage in Memphis* album. I'm just a behind-the-scenes guy, but I was there for a lot of important moments. My name's Barney Stern."

Ryan still had his burger in his hands. He hadn't taken a bite. "Ryan Wyatt."

"Go ahead and eat, kid. You're a growing boy."

Ryan bit into the burger, then placed it on his plate and removed the top bun, scraping the fried onion ring off but leaving the lettuce, tomato, pickles, cheddar, and bacon. He replaced the bun top and took a second bite.

"You're not from here. You on vacation?"

Ryan spoke through his mouthful. "Los Angeles. Here to see Graceland with my girlfriend."

Barney rubbed his hands together. They were large, but the rest of him was spindly and thin. "Good, good. How old are you?"

"Eighteen. Just graduated."

"Got any plans?"

"College, eventually."

The old man smiled. "Bet you can sing."

"A little bit."

"Give me a few bars of a song."

A bit of sliced tomato fell out of Ryan's mouth. Was this guy serious?

"What? You're shy? Let's go to the john."

Ryan was still staring at him.

Barney broke into a crafty smile. "Don't worry, kid. I'm not some old perv. Consider it an audition."

Ryan put his burger back on his plate, wiped his hands, and followed the old man to the restroom, when the old man leaned against the wall and waited. With *Blue Hawaii* fresh in his mind, Ryan began to sing *Can't Help Falling in Love*.

A toilet flushed, and a man came out of a stall. He gave them both a look, washed his hands, and left, but Ryan didn't stop singing. Barney's attention was rapt, his sharp eyes gleaming.

At song's end, the old man applauded and grinned, his teeth as yellow as hundred-year-old piano ivories. "Rock-A-Hula, Baby!"

"Rock-A-Hula," Ryan replied, taking a slight bow.

The old man fumbled in his pocket. He pulled out a wilted wallet and removed a business card, extending it toward Ryan with an unsteady hand.

"If you ever feel like seeing the world, call this guy. He'd hire you in a second. Tell him Barney recommended you. I don't say that to all the kids. You gotta have charisma and talent and, buddy, you've got it, without a speck of doubt."

Ryan accepted the card without looking at it.

Barney wasn't done. "Talent like yours is authentic, and to me, anything authentic is the truth. You know what the King said about the truth?"

Ryan shook his head and held the bathroom door for the old man, allowing him to totter ahead of him.

Barney stopped outside the restroom and rested his ancient claw on Ryan's arm. "Truth is like the sun. You can shut it out, but it ain't going away."

46

Dan and Ron escorted Marilyn out to her topless MG, squeezed into half a space near the elevator on the third floor of the hospital parking structure.

On the way, she told the cousins about her return trip from PPP that morning. A bright yellow Ford Focus ST followed her onto the northbound 101, so she kept an eye on her rearview mirror as she merged from the slow lane to the fastest one far left, next to the carpoolers. After a mile of industrial buildings, Section 8 housing developments, factories, fields, cement walls, overpasses, and on-ramps, the Focus joined her in the fast lane, two cars back. After another mile passed, she slid across the lanes back into the slow lane to see if he'd follow her. After half a mile, he crept in next to her and then scooted directly behind her. Startled, she moved into the middle lane, and he followed. Cutting back, he followed again. There was a break in the glut of traffic, so she careened all the way from the slow lane into the fast lane, then back again, and the Focus followed.

The sound of a police siren pierced the noise of the traffic. Blue lights strobed in her rearview mirror, and the officer used his loudspeaker to command her to pull over. Chastened, Marilyn slid over to the guardrail on the shoulder and waited. The door on the driver's side of the police car slammed, and she watched in her side mirror as a beefy African-American cop made his way toward her car, pausing at her rear bumper, bending down as if to inspect something. It took half a minute for him to rise to his full height of six-foot-six and approach the driver's side. "License and registration."

She grabbed her pocketbook. Past the tissues, gum, makeup, scraps of paper, loose coins, and Bic pens, she found the pouch she kept her identification in. Unzipping it, she flipped past her credit cards until she came to her license.

"And registration."

With a sigh, she leaned over to open her glove box.

"Slowly," he warned.

She pulled out the paperwork and handed it to him.

"I'll be right back."

"Can I just ask—" she began.

His response was a glance over his shoulder. She pushed the eject button on her CD player, removed Coldplay's *Mylo Xyloto*, and put the disc back into its case. Ahead, up the freeway, the Focus was parked on the shoulder beneath an underpass.

A chill ran through her. *Who is that?*

The officer returned to her window and handed back her license and registration. His nametag said "Griffin." He took two steps back and began writing a ticket.

Marilyn was aghast. "What did I do?"

"Failure to signal when changing lanes."

"What? No one does that."

"Then they should all be fined. Including you."

"Someone was chasing me. They're driving a yellow Focus."

Griffin stopped writing on his pad. "Oh?"

"They're right up—" Marilyn searched the shadows beneath the underpass.

"Right up where?"

"Up there. They were parked and waiting."

"Have you been drinking?"

"No. I'm telling you the truth."

Griffin surveyed the empty stretch of shoulder, then tore the ticket off his pad and handed it to her. Marilyn felt like crumpling the ticket and throwing it at him.

"What do I do if they come back? Maybe it's road rage. Maybe I cut them off and they're going to shoot me."

The cop almost cracked a smile. "If you see your imaginary yellow Focus again, here's my card." He passed it to her and began to walk away.

Marilyn studied it. Alan Griffin was a sergeant with the LAPD.

Dan and Ron stood by the trunk of Marilyn's car and listened to her story. When she was done, Dan hunkered down and felt beneath her bumper. "You say the cop bent down around here?"

Marilyn nodded. "But I don't think he put anything under there. He's a cop."

When Dan stood up, he held a tiny black device in his hand. "You don't, huh?"

Ron was excited. "Let me see that."

Ron examined the device while Dan grinned at Marilyn.

Even though she knew the answer, she asked, "Is that like one of ours?"

Ron pointed to a serial number alongside the magnetic strip. "LAPD."

Dan chuckled. "Deep."

Marilyn asked another question she knew the answer to. "Why track me?"

Dan ran his fingers along his thumb, suggesting money was at play. "I think at least a cop or two are in Bertrand's pocket."

Ron walked three cars down and stuck the tracking device beneath the bumper of an off-duty United taxi cab. "This should keep them running all over town."

47

There was no need to enter the room quietly when Ryan made it back to the hotel. Bea was sitting up in bed, watching Elvis sing about the warden throwing a party in the county jail.

Ryan held up the container, announced he'd brought her food, and then proceeded to come over to her bed and open the Styrofoam box so she could see what was inside. Her eyes lit up. He'd brought her a honey citrus grilled chicken salad topped with all kinds of goodies from blue cheese to spiced pecans to orange slices to red pepper strips to dried cranberries. She picked at the lid on the four-ounce cup of dressing and poured it liberally across the top of the bed of grilled Cajun chicken and greens. Ryan dug inside the white bag and came up with a plastic fork and three napkins. After handing them to her, he went and sat down at the end of her bed to watch her eat. Her hair was damp with sweat, hanging in droopy hanks that now appeared light brown. Her eyes looked tired, but she was smiling. She didn't need to ask where he'd been. The bag had the Hard Rock Café logo on it.

"Did you have fun?"

Ryan got up to turn down the volume on the TV and paused, captivated by what he saw. Elvis and his boys did a choreographed dance, and Ryan marveled at the King's fluid movements. "How does he stay up on his toes like that? I really need to practice my dancing more."

"And if you can't find a party, you're gonna have to partner with wooden chair."

"What about you?"

Bea picked at her salad. "My dancing days might be over."

Ryan was sorry he'd said anything. He sat down on the bed again and watched as she bit into a forkful of chicken. "Is it good?"

She nodded. "Thanks. Sorry I was sleeping. I didn't know I was so tired."

"It's understandable."

"You never answered my question. Did you have fun?"

Ryan thought about the business card from Barney Stern in his wallet and debated whether or not he should tell her about it. Realizing he never kept any secrets from her, he decided to pull out his billford and remove it from the slot he'd tucked it in.

"Met a guy about as old as Larry King. Kind of even looked like him."

"Jeez. What did you have to talk about?"

"He had me sing for him in the bathroom and said I have the right stuff. Then he gave me this."

He passed the card to her and she squinted at it. "Bacchanalia Cruises? I don't get it."

Ryan thought he did. He knew cruise lines hired performers for their lounge acts, and for a split second, he imagined himself sailing away from the Port of Los Angeles off the San Pedro Pier. The breezes would invigorate him, the waters would dazzle him, and either direction he went—south to Baja or north to Vancouver—promised untold adventures. The deep purple lounge would be filled with thirty round tables, each seating four.

There would be a Madonna impersonator strutting the stage in a conical bra, an old dude doing Frank Sinantra tunes, and himself, singing to a hound dog plushie.

He felt movement on the bed and his reverie burst like a champagne bubble. Bea got up and rushed to the bathroom. He heard the toilet lid slam against the porcelain tank as she raised it. Then he heard violent retching.

Jumping up, he ran into the bathroom and knelt down beside her. She was on her knees with her head so far over the rim of the toilet her face was nearly in the vomit.

Gently, he lifted her long hair away from the bowl and held it back from her clammy neck.

When her stomach was empty, she turned to smile apologetically. "I took extra meds so I could keep up with you on this trip, but I think I took too many."

Ryan kissed her forehead.

"You don't need to keep up with me," he told her. "I'm here for you."

48

Violet Tearlach considered herself blessed. Her programmer boyfriend had found a backdoor into Gmail, Hotmail, and Yahoo so she could track what celebrities were saying in theoretically private correspondence and then sell the dirt to the tabloids. She was busy telling Marilyn how Kerr MacNaghten's father was trying to convince his son to get rid of the five hundred live hand grenades he kept in his basement when Marilyn's second line rang and a mysterious caller promised he'd tell her about Betrand's plans to destroy her if she met him alone at a motel in Venice.

Though the place was called Penny's Rose Garden, the place had less to do with scents than cents. The path from the sidewalk to the lobby was embellished with pennies set in concrete before it dried. Bored or greedy grubbers had pried a couple out, which Marilyn thought was a lot of work.

With floor to ceiling glass windows, the lobby also featured penny-embellished adornments from lamps to corner tables, from the front door to the check-in counter. Though the man at the desk wore a stovepipe hat and his nameplate read "A. Lincoln," he was overweight and blond.

At least he has a beard. "Abe?" She tapped her nails, which she had painted Le Vernis Sky Line, on the counter.

The man looked embarrassed. "No. Andrew. But at least another great president, Andrew Jackson was."

"I'm supposed to get a key for 104. My named is Marilyn Coffey. Or Nicole. Depends on what he told you."

He raised his eyebrows. "Right. Already pre-paid."

He stood there, looking at her.

Come on, Abe, clock is ticking.

He cleared his throat. "Do you like looking like Marilyn? That woman was so sad."

"Marilyn was sad?"

"I just think a person should try to look like themselves, and especially not try to look like someone who was used by men, had virtually no talent, relied on her looks, and overdosed on pills."

Marilyn gave Abe a strange look. She did have a few things in common with the real Marilyn, both in the being-used-by-men department and not being appreciated for her talent. "Not that it's any of your business, but I'm trying to change that. Do you like looking like Abraham Lincoln?"

Abe avoided her eyes and gave her a room key and a map that showed the location of the room. "Doors face out, sliding glass doors face the inner courtyard. And we have a nice pool."

Marilyn thanked him and followed the path of pennies around the corner. The hollow door opened with a key rather than a key card, another quaint but charming feature of the aging hostelry.

Inside, the room was as unpredictable as other aspects of the motel. A mass-produced reproduction of Joseph Mallord William Turner's *The Slave Ship*, from 1840, hung over the bed, and Marilyn wondered if the image of slaves drowning in choppy waters while their ship sank was conducive to a guest's restful stay. She imagined it was chosen for its abolitionist stance, since it tied in with the Lincoln era and the President's eventual call to end slavery in 1864.

The Civil War era and thoughts of an artist considered "a painter of light" long before Thomas Kinkade protected that phrase through trademark and churned out self-proclaimed masterpieces of Hansel and Gretel cottages lit from within by cozy fires made Marilyn feel bone tired. She threw her handbag on the bed and stared at the bedside lamp-base busts of Mary Todd Lincoln and Honest Abe. She wondered which bedside drawer held Gideon's Bible, wagered it would be the President rather than his wife, checked his drawer first, and she was right.

She retrieved her cell phone and dialed Graham because she knew he, of all her friends, would put her situation in perspective as only a Brit could. Someone should know where she was in case anything went wrong.

He picked up on the second ring and said hello just loud enough to be heard over the noisy street traffic.

"Where the hell are you, G?"

"Answering the phone while driving on the 5. Why, you—"

The door to the room clicked shut.

She turned to see who it was but didn't recognize the man.

"Hang up now and turn your phone off," he told her.

Marilyn pretended to punch the button that would terminate her connection with Graham and threw her cell phone into her bag.

49

A line for the shuttle bus to Graceland was forming as, off to the side, visitors were having their pictures taken in front of a pictoral backdrop depicting the famous Graceland gates and, beyond them, the tan limestone mansion. Ryan begged Bea for a souvenir shot of the two of them together, but Bea declined. She still wasn't feeling well, was pale, and had only taken her meds after a breakfast of pancakes and eggs a half hour earlier.

The shuttle took less than half a minute to make its way across the street to the thirteen-acre estate. Herded off the shuttle bus, Ryan, Bea, and the other tourists swept past the four Temple of the Winds columns and the lions to the front door, where the guide kept everyone in suspense by drawing out the story of the home's history.

Bea wanted to sit down but opted for leaning against Ryan, who held her steady. Inside, it was everything they expected. Facing the mirrored white staircase, the guide called their attention to rooms on the right—the living room with a sofa that seemed unusually long and, beyond that, a doorway framed on both sides with stained glassed artwork depicting peacocks that led into the music room, where a mid-century television set and a black baby grand remained.

Ryan looked down at the guardrail preventing entry and grimaced.

"Look but don't touch," he whispered to Bea.

She offered him a wan smile.

The tour continued with a look at Elvis' parents' bedroom, which was blindingly white from the walls to the carpet, except for the queen-sized bed that was covered with a grape-colored velour spread. Bea pointed at the glassed-in closet where some of Gladys Presley's dresses were displayed. Ryan nodded. He was focused on the pink bathroom off the bedroom that was cordoned off.

As the morning progressed, Bea showed increasing fatigue, and Ryan and she fell behind. A bald-headed man turned around not once, but twice, looking like he wanted to say something to Ryan.

Upstairs, where Elvis died in August 1977, was off-limits. Instead, they were taken through the bar and billiards and media rooms in the basement before heading up to the Jungle Room, where Ryan could easily picture Elvis kicking back and having fun.

Next, they headed across the backyard toward Vernon Presley's office and made their way across the lawn to the trophy room. Bea tugged on Ryan's arm and led him to a white fence that penned in grazing horses.

"What's wrong?" he asked.

Bea sank down into the grass. "I feel a little faint. Maybe it's the humidity."

Ryan watched the group enter the trophy room where Elvis' gold lame suit was on display. The bald-headed man who had given Ryan a second glance broke away from the pack and made his way across the lawn.

"Is something wrong?" he asked. "Do you guys need help?"

Bea tried to smile but failed. "I'm just lightheaded. I need to rest a moment."

The man eyed Ryan. "Guess I don't have to tell you who you look like."

"Yes, I know, and no, I'm not an Elvis impersonator, and I don't have a show in Vegas. Ryan Wyatt."

He stuck out his hand and the man clasped it with his own, his rings flashing.

"Ben Andover. But you can sing, right?"

Ryan debated whether or not he should issue an aw-shucks-maybe reply, then rethought things. He simply said yes.

"How do you feel about Hollywood?" Ben asked.

Ryan laughed. "Considering we're from Beverly Hills?"

"Oh!" The man sounded surprised.

He pulled a business card from his billfold and handed it to Ryan.

"What's this?"

"They're having auditions for a new singing competition called *The It Factor* on the Lynx Network. The competition runs twelve weeks. It would give you a lot of exposure. Plus, if you win, you get a record contract. When are you going back?"

"We're only in Memphis this weekend," Ryan told him.

"Great," Ben said. "Auditions are this coming Wednesday at the Rose Bowl in Pasadena. Think you can make it?"

Ryan looked at Bea, uncertain.

Bea rallied a real smile.

"You've got to try out," she told him. "I'll be mad at you if you don't."

Ben laughed and returned his billfold to his back pocket. "Guess you better listen to the little lady."

Ryan helped Bea back to her feet.

"I always do."

50

Ron Fletcher and Logan Lockhart sat in Peter Corcioni's office on the sixtieth floor of one of the Marina City towers on Chicago's State Street, waiting for the old man to conclude a meeting. Both wore plaid shirts, jeans, and sneakers. Ron had gelled his dark hair flat, combed straight back from his forehead, and Logan slightly modified his fauxhawk so that it spiked to the left. After Ron checked his iPhone for messages and logged into Gmail to find out if anyone had written, his attention turned to Corcioni's trove of CIA spy gear, displayed in barrister cabinets throughout his thirty-foot long executive suite carpeted in oatmeal berber. The tower his friend Phil's father worked in was one of two corncob-shaped buildings that overlooked the main branch of the Chicago River to the south and, beyond that, the Chicago Loop. In the opposite direction, Wrigley Field was a short four and half mile jaunt away, lit up for night games every spring and summer.

Ron wasn't as enthusiastic about the views as he was about Corcioni's gadgets, though, and there was always a new gizmo or two he wanted to ask him about. He knew about the shelf of fake calluses that were used to cover microfilm placed against the skin, and another shelf that contained men's smoking pipes with cavities that had been hollowed out to hide information. There was a shelf filled with pens containing invisible ink so messages could be written on a spy's skin, and beside them were a handful of false glass eyes, bleached and painted inside so they could hold information. Then there was a shelf filled with stacks of thick foreign currency that had been boiled apart so microdots of information could be put inside the bill, typically in a spot where the bill was darker, before it was glued back together. Beside the paper money, there were stacks of coins with tiny holes in them. If you put a needle into the hole in any coin, you could pop it open like a tin of Altoids.

Ron waved Logan over to join him before he lifted the glass door on the bill and coin cabinet and reached for a coin that sat apart from the neat stacks, closest to the stacks of bills. He held it up to the light before he reached into his pocket to retrieve his bifocals. While Ron gazed at the coin, his concentration was so deep he didn't hear his friend's father enter the room.

"Going blind like me, I see?"

Ron gave a start and turned. "Still quiet as a fox, old man?"

They hugged and examined each other at arm's length before Ron introduced him to Logan and explained Logan's condition.

"Can't talk?" the old man asked. "Wish the secretarial pool here had that problem."

"He's our graphics guy," Ron explained, "so if he has any questions about the formats you provide, he has his iPad."

Corcioni led them over to his desk, and Ron asked him how his son Phil was doing as they sat down.

The old man settled into a desk chair impressive enough for the Oval Office. "Are you done with the niceties? I spoke with him last night, and he mentioned you two talked only a few days ago."

Logan thought he was the only one who blushed until he watched Ron's face flush a lovely shade of pink.

Corcioni pulled out a pipe and a pouch of tobacco while Ron composed himself, unlatched his briefcase, and pulled out his laptop. He opened the layout of the first issue Logan had done and slid it across the massive desk to Corcioni, who took a puff on his pipe, leaned forward, and looked.

"She wants them to look like NetFlix mailers with perforated edges."

The old man shushed him.

Ron dug around in his briefcase and pulled out a sample first issue from PPP that Marilyn had given him. He pushed it across the desk, but Corcioni ignored it.

While they waited ten minutes, Ron entertained Logan by sharing stories Corcioni had told him about dead drops. Forested areas were always good. You could use a hollowed-out branch or, better yet, a hollow spike with a capped lid you'd insert into the ground and step on till the cap was flush with the ground and virtually undetectable. You could even use garbage and stuff a message written on a napkin into the bottom of a cup, returning it to the refuse bin or tossing it on the ground with other litter. Good dead drops lasted for hours. In the event of problems, you could leave chalk marks to signal to an agent there was a change of plans. But the biggest thing to consider when sizing up a suitable dead drop was realizing you had to have a reason for being there. While there wasn't much call for wandering around the woods at night, a far better choice for a drop was an underground parking garage filled with cars. It was simply a matter of getting out of your car, getting into the car of the person you were meeting, exchanging information, and then parting ways. As a paparazzo, this was Ron's preferred method of meeting sources.

Corcioni looked across the desk. "We can do this, no problem."

Ron beamed. "With the perforation and everything?"

"Right here in Chi-Town."

Corcioni had taken advantage of the fact *The Chicago Sun-Times* had stopped the presses, closed its printing plant, laid off four hundred employees at its South Ashland Avenue facility, and moved to the Freedom Center downtown. There was equipment to be had in the transfer, and he made haste to secure what he could for his firm.

"She's gonna want to know how much."

"With distribution?"

"Yep." Marilyn had filled Ron in on what to ask for, what to get.

"What's your price point?"

"She wants them to go cheap so they're an impulse purchase. Thirty-five cents, tops."

"Tell her to lower it to a quarter. I can run these at five cents each, with distribution of a hundred thousand copies to ten major cities coast to coast, and get them on the racks at the registers right next to *The National Enquirer*. That's ten thousand issues per city, with leftovers being picked up when trucks deliver the next one. You got any more issues besides this first one?"

Ron came around and looked over the old man's shoulder. As a cloud of sweet cherry-smelling smoke enveloped them,

Ron showed him a list of stories in the making Marilyn had given him.

"Good, good. Keep 'em coming. We've got trucks going out every day. If you've got the stories, we could theoretically do seven runs a week."

"And you really can get them on the racks near checkouts, right next to *The Enquirer*?"

Corcioni looked up at Ron, his thick neck swallowed by a cashmere turtleneck that nearly ran up the underside of his chin. "Kid, you ever hear of a little thing called connections?"

Ron's iPhone rang. "Yeah, Dan, what's up?"

As he listened, his face fell. He moved to the chair across from Corcioni's desk and sat down hard. After he hung up, he shared the news. "Marilyn was found raped and beaten in Venice. She's alive, but barely. Dan thinks ex-cons hired by *Flash* did it."

Corcioni sucked on his pipe and blew out a plume of smoke.

"*Flash* is where she worked before?"

Logan and Ron nodded simultaneously.

"And she left and took a lot of staff with her?"

"She cherrypicked the best," Ron said.

Corcioni tapped his pipe on the ashtray. "Surprised they didn't kill her. This business—" he stopped and coughed, leaving the sentence unfinished.

51

Because Bea wasn't feeling up to it, Noah accompanied Ryan to *It Factor* auditions at the Rose Bowl in Pasadena, where thousands turned out to audition. The show's host was both hyperactive and charismatic, jumping around onstage, welcoming the throngs. Interns gave everyone a number, and the potential contestants lined up at screening tents set up on the grounds.

After eight hours of waiting, Ryan was granted the chance to sing a few bars of *Love Me Tender* for a team of judges and was greenlighted to meet the star panel. He emerged from the tent, hugged Noah, and pointed to a squat, windowless building that looked like it belonged in Quantico. "We're supposed to go over there."

The two of them crossed the grounds, found seats, and watched Bartelmus Starr roughhouse with little kids. Ryan and Noah were dressed for the hot weather, but the sun was still beating down hard at five in the afternoon and they were a sweaty mess. Finally back to business, Bartelmus approached the boys and read the sticker on Ryan's gold-and-white striped t-shirt. "181-226-343-442-551."

Ryan looked down. Only the first six numbers were on it.

Bartelmus broke into a wide grin. He wore a three-piece suit but still looked as fresh as his newly pressed pocket square. Noah nudged Ryan. Bartelmus was making a joke and they were obliged to laugh.

"Oh, right." He stood up and towered over Bart, who hugged him around the waist. Then, throwing his arms wide as if to welcome Jesus, he flagged down some men with cameras and scrutinized his clipboard again.

The lights from the cameras lit up Ryan and Bartelmus.

Bartelmus spoke directly to the blinking red light on the first camera. "This is Ryan Wyatt, and he's ready to meet the judges. Where are you from, Ryan?"

"Right here in Southern California."

"Specifically?"

"Beverly Hills."

"And you are how old?"

"Eighteen. Nineteen in October."

"Whoa, don't rush it," Bartelmus chuckled. He winked at the red light on the camera. "We get old too fast, don't we?"

The middle-aged viewership must love this little leprechaun, Ryan thought.

Bartelmus looked at him, eyes wide. "So, are you nervous?"

Ryan shrugged. "Not really."

Still seated in his folding chair, Noah spoke up. "He does a lot of karaoke."

The cameras swung wide to include Noah, dressed in a solid blue shirt and denim shorts, his sandy hair matted with sweat. The pride and admiration he felt for his friend was written all over his sunburned face. Bartelmus took a seat beside him, grabbed his hand and pumped it. "You're here for Ryan?"

"Yes. I'm his friend."

"And your name?"

"Noah. Noah Che—"

Bartelmus didn't let him finish. He dropped Noah's hand as though he'd been grasping something unsavory and jumped back up. He grabbed Ryan again and led him to the crouched concrete building that looked like it was trying to hide from its prey. Bartelmus pointed toward the shiny metal door. The cameras were tracking them.

Bartelmus looked serious, but his words carried a lilt, suggesting hope.

"This is it, kid."

"This is it," Ryan parroted. He rubbed his hands together.

"Go get 'em, and good luck."

52

When Marilyn was released from the hospital, she had Tobias drive her straight home, where she stayed in bed, beneath her white goose comforter for days, in a haze of painkillers. On the seventh day, Pia and Tobias stopped hovering, decided she would be okay for a few hours—especially in light of the three new locks on the front doors of their adjoining apartments—and left. That afternoon, however, someone began pounding on the door, and Marilyn jolted upright, her heart battering in terror.

Then, just as abruptly as the pounding began, it stopped.

She opened the door to her bedroom and looked out.

In her purse on the bed, her cell phone rang to the tune of *Diamonds Are A Girls Best Friend.* She answered it.

"Marilyn?"

"Yes?" She didn't recognize the caller's voice, which frightened her further.

"This is Tom. The security agency sent me over so you could interview me."

Still on the phone, Marilyn crept to the front door and peered through the peephole. An impossibly tall man stood there. She couldn't see his eyes, but he had a strong, square chin.

She noticed a card for Best Bodyguards on the dining room table, and she picked it up, trying to remember what was going on. "I'm gonna hang up and call the agency and verify your identity. What's your name?"

"Tom Nielsen."

She disconnected the call and dialed the number on the card. "Did you send a giant to my place?"

There was laughter on the other end of the line before the woman called over her shoulder to someone else in the room. "How tall is Nielsen?"

"The Dunkin' Dutchman's evil twin is seven-feet-five-inches," a woman in the background shouted.

"The Dunkin' who?"

The woman on the line sighed. "Rik Smits. Indiana Pacers?"

Marilyn shook her head and peeked through the keyhole again. Tom was pacing.

The woman sounded certain. "That's the guy we sent. Did you forget about today's appointment?"

Marilyn unlocked and opened the door, and Tom breezed past her as though he was afraid she'd push him out if he stood in the doorway. He stopped in the middle of her white shag rug and looked down. "Uh, my shoes may be dirty."

Marilyn closed and relocked the door before she crept over to him and looked up. He towered above her and had hair so blond it bordered on white.

She extended her hand. "Marilyn."

He treated her hand as though it were made of fine china. "Tom Nielsen."

"I know. The agency sent you."

He looked around, then at her shirt. "What's Pink+Dolphin? A rock band?"

She didn't hear his question. She sat down on the sofa and felt the bandages on her head. "I must look a mess."

Tom looked down at the waif of a woman, her head swathed in white, both eyes blackened, bandages on her hands, arms, and legs. A wave of pity washed over him.

"I've seen worse," he reassured her, though he knew it wasn't true.

53

Ryan had never seen Crann Berry, Deth Mental, or Tamarind Toxic in person before, but here they were, sitting before him at a long table filled with cups promoting StazUp Cola, the drink that promised to keep you awake not only all night but forty-eight straight. Deth was the token hardcore rocker who nearly died by overdosing throughout the sixties and seventies, only to discover rehab and fidelity with one of Hugh Hefner's pets at the Playboy mansion before the eighties ended. Wearing a full Native American headdress and suede dress for the auditions, he wouldn't even touch the Staz, though he kept the cup right in front of him per the sponsor's request. Instead, he waited for breaks and had his assistant serve him green tea, pistachios, and dried fruit to keep him going. He was the hardass on the panel, the one who said what he thought even if it drove contestants to despair, and there were always a few bad singers included in the mix just so everyone could have a good laugh when Deth ripped them to shreds.

Both female judges were current pop stars. Crann was known for her breathy vocals, scanty costumes, choreography, and conquests. Tamarind was known for her weird Sitar wailing endorsed by Deepak Chopra, Oprah, and New Agers worldwide for its ability to induce trancelike states. That any of them were suited to judge singing talent was questionable, but Ryan was ready to give them a chance.

"Who are you, lad?" Deth asked as Ryan approached the taped marks on the floor.

"Ryan Wyatt. I'm local."

"You ever cut any LPs?"

Ryan shook his head.

"You know who you look like, do you?"

Ryan nodded. "I do. In fact, I'm going to sing one of his songs for you now."

"Right, then," Deth said. "On with it."

There was no musical accompaniment. The auditions were a cappella.

Ryan stood perfectly still, focused, and then launched into *Heartbreak Hotel*. Immediately, he began to gyrate as his singing resounded off the walls. The three judges were captivated. He needed two yeses to make it through to the live shows. As he finished the last line of the song, Tamarind let out an ungodly shriek of approval and stood up. Her chair tipped, fell, and clattered on the floor.

"This is what we've been waiting for," she screamed.

"Wait your turn," Crann said coolly. "I get to comment first."

Deth turned to Tamarind. "She does, you know."

"Sorry. I couldn't help myself."

"Bloody hell," Deth said. "Why don't we all save some time and answer in unison?"

54

As Logan finished each story, he took it upstairs, knocked, and waited for Marilyn to peer through the peephole and open the door. She didn't go out without Tom anymore, and Logan suspected she and her bodyguard had fallen in love.

Today, he came up to tell her the Susannah Byron and Bruce Cedric layout was ready, and like all the spreads he worked on, he easily imagined himself on the scene with Belle and Graham as they trudged up the hill leading to Laurence Conrad's Hollywood

Hills hideaway, an underground fortress reputed to be eco-friendly. Everyone suspected Susannah and her husband Bruce were experiencing marital woes when he failed to meet her at LAX on her return from Czechoslovakia, where she'd been filming *The Red Agenda*. When Marilyn got word that Susannah had hopped into a taxi and wasn't headed home, she was certain the actress was on her way to her lover Laurence's bunker.

"I hear his place is fireproof," Graham commented, trying to keep pace with Belle, who was twenty paces ahead. "Earthquake proof too. *The Star* says his place will still be standing in the year 4000."

Belle stopped to refasten the elastic around the ponytail high atop her head. Black curls tumbled onto her shoulders. "But does he get any sunlight?"

The scrub on the hillside was crisp, dry, and ripe for fire season. It crunched underfoot as they trudged on. "Sure. The living room is wall-to-ceiling glass, exposed to the backyard. Tapped his phone line five years ago." They had reached the summit, where a fence marked Laurence's property line. A dark green hedge of rosemary ran alongside the length of chain-link, and by squatting in the tangled grasses, they could hide from view. Belle found a large rock to sit on, and Graham chose one nearby. He removed his camera from his oversized fanny pack and fiddled with the settings. He pointed his camera toward the back of Laurence's house and focused the lens so he had a clear view of the living room. Within minutes, there was movement inside. Laurence headed to his front door and opened it to greet Susannah, who placed her suitcase on the floor and fell into his arms.

Maybe Logan hadn't been there, but he wished he had been. Living vicariously through stories told by reporters had to suffice, but he fought the nagging feeling he was invisible, expendable, off the radar, not fully alive, less important due to his defect, his inability to engage another living soul in meaningful conversation.

He knocked again, and Marilyn and Tom answered the door in matching *Daily Celebrity* sweatshirts. Her fingers and toes were painted with Chanel le Vernis Orange Blossom, and her newly-chopped hair had grown so flyaway bits covered the tops of her elfin ears and lifted up around wounds that had scabbed. She had left the Monroe look behind and had morphed into someone new: herself. She twirled around and knocked into Tom, who caught and held her, a big smile on his face. Tom, whose father had been in the tabloid game since the earliest days of *The National Enquirer*, liked to play a game with her. He would give her three stories and ask her which one had actually been published back in the eighties, when he was growing up in Laguna Niguel and tabloids were required bathroom reading.

On the way downstairs, with Marilyn riding piggyback, Tom shifted to address her. "Story one. When Johnny Waters dated Charlisse Witherspoon, did he forbid her to wear underwear? Story two. When a guy doing props on Jennifer Dench's movie made a joke about her weight, did she make him write out, *I must not call Jennifer fat* one hundred times on cue cards? Story three. Is there a website dedicated solely to promoting Janet Kimberly Charter's breasts?"

Marilyn nuzzled Tom's neck. "I hate that you're older than me and remember this stuff. Story number one about no underwear is probably true. I don't think anyone could convince a props guy to write anything a hundred times, and, with regard to Charter's breast website, I don't think they had the Internet when you were young."

Tom laughed. "Ouch. And you're right again. Johnny forbade Charlisse to wear underwear, but I don't know how often she complied."

They reached the landing where Logan stood and followed him through the laundry room to his front door made of white particleboard, secured with a flimsy lock.

"All the layout work gets done in his place," Tom pointed out, "and there isn't even an alarm."

"No one's going to look for stuff down here," Marilyn argued.

"Better safe than sorry. Always."

Logan unlocked his door and pushed it inward, moving ahead of them into his small place which consisted of a bed, a tiny stand where he kept a table lamp, a framed photo of the late Professor X and a vial of hair, a forty-pound mini-fridge that served double duty as a surface for his turntable, a bank of computers with office chairs, and a bathroom with a sink, toilet, and shower. The place was dedicated to Elvis, with posters and tin signs hanging on every wall. The eleven-by-twelve-inch wall calendar above the head of his microfleece-blanketed twin bed featured black and white photos of Elvis. This month's picture was of the Million Dollar Quartet, with Elvis seated on a piano bench and Jerry Lee Lewis, Carl Perkins, and Johnny Cash standing behind him, back on December 4, 1956, in Memphis at Sun Record Studios.

While Logan called up the new issue on his dual monitors, Marilyn slid off Tom's back and he launched into another trivia quiz. "Story one. When Felicity Mirren stayed at the Villa Ensoleillé during Cannes, she disliked the room's wallpaper so much she had them cover it up. Story two. When Mickey Bridges went to a feng shui practitioner and was told he was going to father an evil monster, he put a metal board under his mattress to ward off negative energy. Story three. When Heath Phoenix was dating porn star Samantha Castle, he started taking Viagra and claimed they had sex twelve times a day every day until they broke up."

Marilyn snatched the pillow from the head of Logan's bed and hit Tom squarely in the stomach with it. "Story one is true, because there weren't any feng shui practitioners when you were growing up and there sure as hell wasn't any Viagra."

Tom took the pillow away and walloped her with it. "Do you have any idea how old feng shui is?"

"Sure. They invented it when you turned forty, back in the Pleistocene epoch."

Logan waved them over to the monitors. The left screen was a view of the issue's sealed cover. It read, "Who's Cheating Now?" with photos of Susannah Byron, Bruce Cedric and Laurence Conrad in cameo-shaped bubbles surrounding the question.

"Nice cover," Marilyn said, resting her hand gently on Logan's shoulder. She pulled up a chair and examined the photo Graham managed to get of Laurence kissing Susannah by his front door, her suitcase on the floor at her feet. It was a great shot, and the story by Belle and Graham only made it better.

"When Bruce Cedric failed to meet his wife Susannah Byron at the airport in late June when she returned from Czechoslovakia, where *The Red Agenda* was filming, it was a huge clue something might be wrong with their marriage. After all, they hadn't seen each other since April. Didn't he miss her?

"Apparently, not so much. Who's the first man Susannah wanted to see when she touched foot back in the States? Laurence Conrad, Susannah's co-star in *The Near Missus* in 2003.

"How many times has Susannah met with Conrad in his Hollywood Hills bunker? Hard to say, but A-list insiders say their relationship started not long after their first movie together and that they take every opportunity to spend time together whenever Bruce is out of town.

Who will file divorce papers first? After Mr. Cedric gets a load of this top-secret snap, it may, in fact, be him."

Marilyn pushed her chair back from the desk. "We're good to go."

Logan nodded and minimized the cover photo and the story layout. His computer wallpaper was a montage of black and white photos of Elvis from the movie *Jailhouse Rock*, with Elvis in various dance poses, balanced on his tiptoes.

Marilyn joined Tom by Logan's front door.

"What's wrong?" Tom asked. "You look a little down."

Marilyn shook it off. "Nothing," she said. "It's a good story."

Logan looked at her. She'd changed since the rape, just as he changed after he experienced his dad's violent death and his mom's horrifying demise, paralyzed by the knowledge that the men who wanted to find him—the men who knew *he* knew what they looked like—would kill him as easily as they'd shot his father down. The feeling was akin to hanging in a web after envenomation, being wrapped in gauzy silk, unable to move, incognizant of anything but the terrible certainty that the shadow looming overhead was malevolent and slaughterous by nature.

55

The ten *It Factor* contestants moved into a sprawling home above Sunset Boulevard on a Tuesday, and Ryan was given a room with Seth, a bug-eyed kid from Texas who sang as though crabs were clamped to every appendage every time he belted out a ballad.

They had twin beds flanking a large picture window overlooking a pool, where the female contestants worked on their tans when they weren't in session with the show's vocal coaches.

Seth was busy tacking up a poster of Shania Twain while Ryan watched.

"You got a girlfriend, man?" Ryan asked.

Seth jumped off his bed and backed up to see if Shania was hanging straight.

"Yep. Sally Rose."

Seth and Sally. Ryan smiled.

Seth was satisfied with the way the poster looked. "You?"

Ryan nodded. "Grew up with her. Her name is Bea. Short for Beatrice."

"What about your dad? Does he look like Elvis too?"

Ryan shook his head. "No. I was a sperm donor baby. Before she met my dad, my mom wanted to get pregnant and do the single mom thing, so she went to a fertility specialist. I've been trying to figure out who my dad is for a long time."

Seth pulled off one of his cowboy boots and threw it across the room.

"Well, then what we have going on here is gonna be just right for you."

"How so?"

"It's the perfect platform to find him. Millions of people watch this show."

"I never have." Ryan went over to his closet and pulled out his laptop so he could set it up at his desk.

"I can show you last season on the net if you want."

"So after I sing and the judges tell me what they thought, I can look straight at the camera and say, 'By the way, I'm looking for my real dad. If you're an Elvis impersonator or simply look like Elvis and you donated sperm in Las Vegas over nineteen years ago, you might be him, so give me a call'?"

Seth pulled off his other boot and threw it. It landed next to the first one as neatly as if he had placed them together on the floor in front of his dresser.

"No. We do confessionals here. Once a week, they put each of us in a little booth, like one of those at church where the priest absolves you of your sins. You Catholic?"

"Yep, but I never went to confession."

Seth stretched his legs. "Well, confession here is not about sharing what you've done wrong. It's about how you feel about the show and the people here. Even me. You can complain about me if you want."

Ryan plugged his laptop into a power strip. "I wouldn't do that."

"Why not?" Seth asked. "The first thing I'm gonna do is complain about how pretty you are."

56

When the next layout was ready for review, Logan went upstairs to get Marilyn and Tom, but instead, he was invited to join the unofficial meeting being held in Marilyn's bedroom. Just back from a trip north, Belle stood with her back to the window, facing the room, while Graham sat on the hope chest at the foot of the bed. The whiteness of Marilyn's down comforter looked like a snow-covered field, her body creating hills and ridges beneath its weight.

Tom hovered by the door and ushered Logan in.

"Logan came to show you the next spread."

Marilyn nodded and pulled the covers up to her chin, her thoughts meandering. Ron's old roommate's father not only insured distribution of 10,000 copies each to New York City, Los Angeles, Chicago, Houston, Philadelphia, Phoenix, Jacksonville, Indianapolis, Columbus, and Charlotte for a total of 100,000 copies nationwide, but he promised they would be at the register, smack beside the omnipresent *National Enquirer*. At a cost of $500 per city, or $5,000 total, she could expect to recoup her investment and have $20,000 profit per issue, and if she had him run five issues a week and they sold out, she could count on a cool hundred grand. Every year she could count on half a million profit, and once she made enough to retire, she would move to a tropical island, where the cabana boys would tend to her every wish. Such was the dream, but first, she had to survive, and survival meant avoiding anyone connected to *Flash* who wanted her out of the picture. If she were asking for Nepture, Uranus, Saturn, or Jupiter—hell, all of the Jovian planets—she would ask for the biggest, most sensational scoop of the century to fall into her lap, just to rub Neville's and Bertrand's fat noses in her success. But one day at a time.

"You're dressed under there, right, Mar?" Belle asked.

Marilyn shot her a withering look.

"Well, you know, you two..." Belle began, waving her hand from Tom to Marilyn and back again.

Not only could Marilyn's friends not hold falling in love against her, it was impossible not to like Tom. He was fun, quick to clean up after they ate together, and good for Marilyn, whose anxiety lessened a notch whenever he was near.

Marilyn sat up and threw the heavy cover off. The sheet and comforter were now clumped on the vacant side of her bed, and she sat on the top sheet with a pillow propped against the headboard at her back. She was dressed in a spaghetti-strapped t-shirt and shorts, and she wore a new necklace Tom bought her. It was a topaz starburst with a tiny satellite of diamonds on a gold chain, and it sparkled whenever Marilyn turned her head. Matching earrings and a bracelet were next on the list. Tom went over to the bed and picked up the pile, shaking the bedclothes out and neatly folding them. Marilyn watched him adoringly. "Oh, my God. Will you take care of me forever?"

Tom smiled. "Only if you keep playing one, two, three with me."

Graham got up from the hope chest and went to stand beside Belle, who had turned to look out at the sky. Logan moved from the doorway and sat on the hope chest Graham vacated. He was dressed in ecru pants and a black shirt that made his eyes and hair look a shade darker.

Graham was curious. "What's one, two, three?"

Marilyn groaned.

Tom's face lit up. "Tell me which of these three stories are true. One, Jesse Franco wanted to name his daughter Incontinence because he believed it meant *across the world* or *across the continents*. Two, a lady met Adrien Cage on Venice Beach and thought he was homeless because he'd recently lost a lot of weight to appear in *Swastika*. She offered him a sandwich and soda, which he accepted and thanked her for. Three, David Andrew Howard wouldn't do a love scene with Melanie Foster until she agreed to shave her legs."

Graham thought a moment. "Three is true. Howard is totally hung up on grooming."

Tom looked at Marilyn. "How about that? A solid guess without a joke about my age."

Marilyn looked around. "I need a gavel." She paused. "Okay, guys, I just wanted to talk about *DC*. Feeling like I'm a marked woman has turned me into a nervous wreck. We'll keep going, but, I mean . . ." she trailed off, unable to finish.

Tom sat down next to Marilyn and took her hand. "What those men did to you, they left you at death's door. They frightened you, violated you, hurt you, and messed up your head so badly, you think they're around every corner, ready to attack. I should think you'd fight even harder to prove you're not only a success, but that you're able to outdo them and be the best-selling tabloid in the nation. They wanted to squash your spirit, kill your drive, make you quit, but the Marilyn I know and love does not give up. She fights back and wins. Can you imagine what a slap in the face it would be to them if you got the story of a lifetime?"

"What in the world could we scoop that would be *that* big?" She closed her eyes and imagined a million issues flying off the racks at stores and newsstands. "Of course I would be thrilled."

Tom held her tight. "Then that's what you've got to shoot for."

57

The first week of *It Factor* featured James Taylor songs, and the judges told Ryan that his *Fire and Rain* sounded like an Elvis cover. The theme for the show's second week was songs from the sixties, so in blatant defiance, Ryan chose to sing the 1963 Elvis hit song, *(You're The) Devil In Disguise*. His performance was so spot-on, Deth Mental leaned back in his chair, studied him a moment, and then quipped, "I thought they only knew how to clone sheep."

"It's like you're a freakin' hologram of Elvis," Tamarind proclaimed. "You know, like they did in that song with Nat King Cole and his daughter."

"You can't just be a copy of someone," Crann surmised. "You can't change your voice, which is so Elvis it's frightening, but you can put a little twist or spin on things so that you're original. Talk to the coaches. Find your niche in the market. You've got to figure out who you are, and you have to fill a void that we didn't even know existed."

Ryan was beginning to wonder why they had even chosen him for the show. He could sing, plain and simple, and they had liked him when he auditioned, but now he had to figure out things he'd never questioned. The one thing he could figure out, though, was the confessional booth, and he used it to try and find his birth dad. His segment lasted three minutes and aired during the third episode, before he sang *Bridge Over Troubled Water* for Simon and Garfunkel week, which Mental said was in his "wheel house" but was "meant to be sung more tenderly."

The confessional booth was no bigger than a closet and just as dark. Floor lights illuminated Ryan from below, making him look like a kid at camp telling a ghost story with a flashlight held beneath his chin.

"Ryan," the cameraman prompted, "tell us something about you we don't know."

Ryan smiled broadly. If he were in court, the cameraman would be accused of leading the witness.

"You all know by now that my name is Ryan Wyatt, but what you don't know is that I'm not Eugene Wyatt's son. I mean, he raised me, but technically he's not my dad. My mom was artificially inseminated in Vegas in '88, and I was born that October. The doctor's records are confidential, but now that I'm eighteen, I feel it's my right to know who my birth father is. Actually, I've always felt it was my right, but considering I'm older and have graduated high school, I feel it's more imperative than ever to meet him and get to know him if I can. If any of you out there see a resemblance between us and you donated sperm to Las Vegas Fertility Associates on Harmon in Vegas at any point during the eighties or earlier, please contact me through the *It Factor* message boards."

He stopped and the cameraman did too.

Ryan's palms were damp, so he wiped them on his jeans. "What'd you think?"

The cameraman rubbed his bearded chin. "It's better stuff than that country rock gal Candy Klymer thinking it's a big secret her favorite color is pink and she collects stuffed unicorns."

58

Logan had three single-story issues to prepare for the coming week, so he turned on the TV for background noise and set to work with a heavy heart. His uncle's health was declining after a series of strokes, and Logan braced himself for the worst. Nancy was with Wendall in the hospital in Vegas, where he was battling pneumonia, and she promised to call Logan the minute she needed him to drop everything and make the final trip to say good-bye.

In the years since Logan discovered the paperwork listing Zella Stuart and Elvis Presley as Ryan's biological parents, he'd been weighed down by the knowledge. Though it secretly thrilled him to know the King had a son with appreciable talent, he also knew he couldn't betray the confidentiality agreement his uncle honored. But once his uncle passed, would it be possible to tell Ryan then? Part of him wanted to, and it was that part that motivated him to win an online auction for clippings of Elvis' hair saved by Homer "Gil" Gilleland, the King's personal hairdresser from early on, into the seventies. The unlabeled amber vial he kept on his bedside table had enough of Elvis' hair for a number of DNA tests and came with a signed certificate of authenticity. It had cost him the sale of his graphic-arts school graduation gift, a '54 Caddy the color of lemon meringue, like one Elvis purchased in 1955. The car was a beauty and Logan loved it, but his last year at *Flash*, he listed it on Craigslist, sold it, and started taking the bus every day. The money he turned over to the auction house was worth every strand of the King's hair they shipped him in return.

He played it through countless times. He would find Ryan, tell him who his father was, and get a hair sample from him so a lab could confirm the truth. Waiting for the lab results might be excruciating, but ultimately, they would get that envelope in the mail, read the letter and, with tears in their eyes, pop the cork on a bottle of champagne and celebrate.

This scenario alternated with another Logan envisioned. Logan would find Ryan and be unable to tell him. The vial of hair in his pocket, he would freeze, unable to move as Ryan got into his car and drove away. He would try again and again, whenever he found the courage, but he could never bring himself to approach the young man who had come to his home so long ago and treated him like a friend. His uncle's confidentiality regarding the matter would loom too large, and Logan would not be able to betray him.

In the end, Logan realized, whatever ultimately happened would hinge on how he felt once his uncle had passed, and he did not look forward to losing the man who had been more like a father to him than his own.

Leaving those thoughts for now, Logan turned to the task of creating a layout for Tobias' story about Helen Hester's daughter's alleged suicide.

That final day at *Flash,* Logan threw his backpack into the back seat of Tobias' black Fiat Croma, placed his iPad on the seat beside him, and combed his fingers through his hair so his faux hawk spiked to full height as Tobias peeled away from the curb.

Fifteen minutes later, they were settled at Tobias' reserved table at The Topiary on Beverly Boulevard, Logan sipping a cup of scalding black coffee and Tobias stirring two Splenda and a non-dairy creamer into his java as Helen Hester arrived. She had been cast as the wife on a new TV show reminiscent of *The Brady Bunch*, complete with blended families comprised of three sons and three daughters, but this time around, it was the mom who brought the sons to the union and the dad who brought the daughters. She even looked a bit like the *Bunch's* Florence Henderson, with big blue Bambi eyes, short blond hair, and a porcelain complexion.

Tobias intended to draw her into a discussion on her cast mates, particularly the actor cast as her husband, who allegedly, like Robert Reed, was gay. He wagered her personal life might be off-limits. She was grieving the loss of her daughter three weeks earlier and coping with nasty gossip that Elen, who'd been single, had been pregnant at the time she'd taken her life.

Befitting her station as a TV mom, Helen wore a cashmere sweater, pearls, dark slacks, and sensible shoes. When the waiter approached the table, she told him she'd like coffee, and two minutes later, he brought it back with three menus. Tobias introduced her to Logan, explained that he was mute, and Helen smiled and took Logan's hand in greeting. Feeling self-conscious, Logan opened his menu and studied it like notes for an important test.

Ultimately, Logan pointed at the tuna melt, Tobias selected fish tacos, and Helen ordered a Caesar salad. Then, sipping their coffee, they enjoyed a moment of silence as they took in their surroundings. Tobias was seated next to the Pegasus topiary, its wings wire-sculpted with tiny points at each tip.

"Pretty, isn't it?" Helen murmured.

"It is. And it's good to see you, Helen. I didn't know if you'd be up to coming out so soon after..."

The unfinished sentence hung in the air. Tobias pulled out his Panasonic recorder and placed it in the center of the table between them. "You mind?"

"No. How else can I be sure I won't be misquoted?"

Tobias frowned, and his expression made her laugh. "I'm kidding. You've always stuck to the facts in stories you've written about me."

"Your TV husband Silas, is he gay like Robert?"

Logan blushed and kept his eyes on his plate, where his half-eaten melt lay unfinished.

"He's 100 percent hetero. In the bedroom scene we did the other day, he actually groped me under my nightgown."

"What'd you do?"

"Hey, any attention an old broad like me can get at this point, the better."

Tobias was incredulous. "You're what, thirty-eight?"

Helen reached across the table, resting her hand on his. "Forty-two."

"So no gay co-star. Any tension on set between the kids?"

"No, they get along great." Helen reached for her napkin and dabbed at her cheek before looking across the restaurant. She seemed to be staring at a topiary sculpture resembling a brontosaurus, but her gaze was unfocused. Tobias contemplated making a joke about the Montauk Monster, but when Helen looked back across the table, her jaw trembled and her eyes filled with tears. "I need to talk to you."

A tear rolled down Helen's cheek and Tobias resisted the impulse to wipe it away. He kept his hands folded, the consummate professional. "I'm listening."

Her jaw trembled again but she began to talk, and by the time their meal arrived, Tobias was embroiled in the actress's search for the truth about her daughter's death, and all Logan could do was sit there and wish he could be more like his friend, asking questions and getting answers. *Aloud.*

The next day, Logan stood beside Tobias on the second story veranda of an apartment complex in West Hollywood and waited for Helen Hester to arrive. The building reminded Logan of a refurbished Motel 6, with concrete staircases that led to upstairs rooms, and a small, gated pool out front, near the street. The sky was cloudless, much as it was the day of Helen's daughter's death. That's what Tobias' online research regarding weather on the eighth told him, as well as the fact it had been seventy-five degrees in West Hollywood between one and three p.m, the estimated timeframe as to when the young woman died.

Apartment 210 had a front window facing the balcony where the men stood, but the curtains had been drawn. The draperies were lined with muslin-colored fabric, creating a blank slate. The inset windowsill held none of the bric-a-brac piled in neighbors' windows—no toys, remotes, keys or snow globes.

Tobias ran a finger around the inside of his collar. He had worn a dress shirt and the morning sun was heating the air, casting shafts of light in shadowed corners. Despite the promise of hot weather, Tobias was glad he had dressed better than usual for his meeting with Helen. The last thing he wanted to do was show up in his usual t-shirt, jeans, and sandals in a situation that required tact, solemnity, and respect. Following Tobias' cue, Logan pulled on the rumpled suit he had worn to the hospital, and even though he paired it with a white t-shirt, he looked presentable.

When she finally arrived, Helen parked her Lincoln Continental near Tobias' Fiat Croma. They watched her swing her legs out of the car and rise with the grace of an aging dancer. Dressed in pale blue, the silk scarf that covered her head fluttered in the lightest breeze.

59

As she reached the top of the landing where they stood, Logan noticed Helen seemed paler than she had at The Topiary. The official inquiry into her daughter's death was closed, but the grief in Helen's eyes when she lifted her prescription sunglasses off her face was palpable. She rummaged through her leather handbag and pulled out a ring of keys with a tiny teddy bear attached. She held it up. "Her keys. I gave her the teddy bear keychain when she got her license. Of course, I got her a Mercedes, too, but only the keychain survived."

Her laugh was rueful. She unlocked the front entrance and the hinges creaked as she pushed the weathered door inward. She waved Tobias and Logan forward, but Tobias stood still and Logan took a step backward.

"Ladies first," Tobias told her.

She went in cautiously, like a kid entering a haunted house, and turned back to face them right away, as though afraid they might change their minds and leave.

They didn't. Logan stepped over the threshold and took a look around. The living room was faux Victorian, with scarlet drapery, a plum velvet-cushioned couch, a glass-topped coffee table, and a piano.

Tobias entered and walked over to the Steinway and examined the sheet music, which was mostly Bacharach and modern pop tunes from the sixties to the present.

"Did she play well?"

Helen joined him and ran her hands lightly over the dusty keys. "Very well. She took lessons and played at recitals. She didn't like classical music much, though."

Logan stepped into the tiny kitchen area and saw toast crumbs on the counter near the toaster. There were photos on the fridge. One woman repeatedly showed up in shot after shot, and she was a miniature version of Helen, complete down to the blond hair, Bambi eyes, and closed-mouth smile.

Tobias was at his elbow. "This her?"

"Yes," Helen said, from behind them.

Tobias zeroed in on a photo where Elen was seated on a young man's lap. They both raised beer bottles to the person taking the picture, their faces touching as they leaned in close. "This the boyfriend?"

"Cody, yes. It's not that I didn't like him. It's just that I—well, I thought Elen could have done better."

Tobias straightened up and left the kitchen, with Helen and Logan trailing after him. After he glanced into the bathroom and the hall closet, he went into Elen's bedroom, where Elen's alleged suicide had taken place. Tobias hoped he could ease into addressing Elen's death gracefully and asked for permission before he sat down on the foot of the bedspreaded queen. Logan took the chair at the desk overlooking the lot behind the building, a view offering nothing more than apartment buildings and trees. He stared out the window intently nonetheless, as though the scenery held clues if he just looked hard enough.

Palms upward on his lap in a gesture of supplication, Tobias was silent. He knew Helen would talk when she was ready. After two minutes of listening to crows squabble on nearby rooftops and watching squirrels tightrope across power lines, Logan turned his attention toward Helen as she began to tell her story.

"Elen took this place when she turned eighteen. She loved being on her own, loved the freedom to do what she wanted. She had an agent and landed parts on *Criminal Minds* and *Cold Case*. Don't know if you've seen her on TV."

Tobias shook his head and Helen continued. "She didn't want to use the last name Hester, said she didn't want anyone saying she was getting free entree into the business because she was my daughter. She used her middle name, James, my maiden name, instead. Two—well, no, three months ago, now—she called me and told me she was pregnant. I was mad, of course, because she said Cody was the father, and I knew he'd never be able to support her, let alone a newborn, so I hung up on her."

Helen's words came slower now. "I called her a few days later, but she didn't answer. Then I sent her a few emails. Again, she didn't answer. So, on the eighth, after a long day on set, I swung by and saw that her new Camry was here. I came up and knocked on her door. She didn't answer. There was a spare key beneath the air conditioner that juts out near her door. Did you see it?"

"The air conditioner?"

"She kept a key tucked in a groove beneath the unit, so I got it and came in." Helen's voice was breaking. "I called her name and came in here. She had a pillowcase over her head and a cord around her neck. I put my head on her chest. There was… nothing."

Tobias was silent for a moment before he spoke. "What was she wearing?"

"What?"

"How was she dressed?

"She was wearing one of those over-sized sleep t-shirts, the kind that go down past your knee. It had a mermaid that looked like a devil on it, and it was orange. I got my cell phone out of my purse and called 911. They were here within fifteen minutes."

She fell silent and Tobias waited. A trickle of sweat ran down the back of his neck.

The apartment was stuffy, and Logan was suddenly aware of a bleachy scent.

When Helen began again, her voice was stronger, as though she'd resolved herself to recount the facts but not feel their import. "When the cops saw she didn't have any defensive wounds on her hands or ligature marks on her wrists, they ruled it a suicide. They said she tied the cord to the upper part of the bed." Helen pointed at one of the posts on the headboard. "And then she laid down and applied pressure to her neck until she asphyxiated."

Tobias cleared his throat, ready to speak, but thought better of it. He recalled Rick Springfield's account of a suicide attempt made in his youth. Springfield fashioned a noose and was going to hang himself in the family's garage. The rope ended up breaking, and Springfield's desire to end his own life was thwarted. But he did say that in those moments when he was losing consciousness, realization of what he was doing kicked in, and the drive toward self-preservation caused him to reconsider his decision. How in the world could someone lie down and quietly suffocate?

"Was Elen taking drugs?"

Helen shook her head. "No. She'd given up antidepressants once she found out she was expecting. I told her it wasn't a good idea to go off Prozac cold turkey and that she should at least ask her doctor about it. But why use the pillowcase?"

"Usually, when someone murders someone they know, they'll cover their victim's face so they don't have to watch what they're doing. Or they'll cover the victim's face later, out of remorse, to hide what they did. You said the rope was *over* the pillowcase?"

"Around its base."

"So the pillowcase wasn't put on afterwards." Tobias couldn't hold back his opinions any longer. "There's no reason to use a pillowcase if you're alone. There aren't any mirrors in here. Elen couldn't see herself and likely wouldn't want to if she could. Someone was with her who didn't want to watch her die because they cared about her."

"There's another thing, too." Helen pointed at the white ceiling fan near the doorway. "She never turned that on. It rattled and she was afraid it was going to come loose, straight out of the ceiling. It was on the day I found her."

Tobias got up and went over to the ceiling fan. He tugged on one of the blades and the fan rattled. Screws around the base were loose, and it had been installed off-kilter. "Excuse me a minute," he told Helen. "Gotta use the facilities, if I may."

Helen nodded and Tobias left the room. Logan and Helen remained there, silent.

The bathroom was tiny; standing in the tub, you could touch both the sink and toilet. There was tissue paper at the top of the trash, so Tobias lifted the mesh canister up to the sink and started sifting through the contents. At the bottom, he found a used pregnancy test stick, the plus sign still visible in its tiny window. Elen had been pregnant, and Helen had lost not only a daughter but a grandchild as well.

If Logan learned a lot by watching Tobias handle Helen's fragile emotions at the restaurant, he learned even more at Elen's apartment. Not jealous in the slightest, Logan only admired the reporter and dreamed he might someday do what Tobias did so well. Now, looking at the story and photos and trying to figure out the best way to present them to readers, he realized that since that day at the apartment, Tobias had accomplished the near impossible and taken the story even farther. For starters, Tobias had obtained the photographs taken at the scene of Elen James' alleged suicide the day her body was found.

Logan used a bold, blocky font for the cover of the issue and typed, "Elen James and Her Unborn Child: Suicide or Murder?" Around the question, he scattered thumbnail photos of Elen, her boyfriend Cody, detectives in charge of the investigation, a photo of the discarded pregnancy test stick, and Helen. The photo inside, which ran flush with the story, showed Elen lying on her bed, dressed in a long shirt, a pillowcase over her head, a cord around her neck. It was gruesome but effective.

"She's every bit the Brady Bunch-type matriarch, Helen Hester is," Tobias wrote, "from her big Bambi blues to her flawless complexion, but what happens when the ultimate icon of all things maternal loses her own child? What happens when detectives tell America's most-loved television mom that her daughter killed herself when, in fact, her daughter had everything—including an unborn child—to live for? And what happens when one of the detectives who deemed the daughter's death a suicide is a mother herself—of the very young man who fathered the woman's child? Confused yet? You should be as confused as the investigation surrounding this suspicious death itself.

"When rumors surfaced that Elen might be pregnant at the time she took her life, Helen hit a roadblock when she attempted to verify that information with the coroner's office. She was told that anything concerning the case was privileged information and couldn't be released, not even to family members, because the death scene was atypical. Elen had called Helen weeks earlier to say she was with child, but Helen wasn't sure if Elen was positive. Having the coroner share his findings would have meant a lot, but officials declined to be forthcoming.

"Elen's final neighborhood in West Hollywood remains quiet, shaded by large trees. Parked cars line the roads due to a shortage of off-street parking. It's a short flight of stairs up to her second-story apartment where, for all the heavy drapery and furnishings, one might guess a Victorian spinster lived. An upright piano sits in one corner, dusty, with Bacharach on the stand. There are still crumbs on the kitchen counter, where Elen loved to butter toast. There is a photo on the fridge of Elen and her boyfriend Cody, smiling at the camera. The rest of the place is small—just a bathroom, hall closet, and bedroom. In the room where Elen slept, the bed is queen-sized and the desk and chair are simple. These are the only furnishings here. And this is where Elen died.

"According to West Hollywood Police Department records, she tied the cord to the upper part of the bed and laid down, applying pressure to her neck until she asphyxiated. The problem with this assumption is that her body would have rebelled in those final moments when the drive to survive kicked in. There is no evidence Elen was impaired, either by drugs or alcohol. She had been excited by the prospect of becoming a mother. She was in love with the baby's father. She had a promising career. Why would she be driven to despair?

"As it turns out, Helen never needed the coroner to confirm her late daughter's pregnancy. At the bottom of the wastebasket in the bathroom, beneath crumpled tissue, there was a used pregnancy test stick investigators overlooked.

"It was positive, as positive as Helen Hester is that her daughter was murdered and that the son of a certain West Hollywood detective may be guilty of homicide."

The layout was done. Logan hit the print button and thought about making coffee. Then his phone buzzed. It was 5:01 a.m., which meant it could only be Nancy.

60

It took a week for Ryan to get two responses, one from an Elvis impersonator in Vegas and one from a lawyer in Colorado. Both were willing to fly to Los Angeles to meet him. Seth insisted on joining Ryan the night of the arranged get-together, so they settled into a C-shaped booth at Boa Steakhouse on Sunset and ordered a pitcher of margaritas while they waited.

The lawyer from Colorado was the first of the two men to arrive. Will Mesmer looked enough like Elvis to be Ryan's dad, but seemed too slender and his complexion too ruddy to be a completely solid physical match. He was in his fifties, his hair was dark blond fading to gray at the temples, and he wore a suit Gene Wyatt would have loved to add to his collection—a gray wool Dolce & Gabbana with a white dress shirt and striped tie. A criminal defense attorney for more than twenty years, Will told Ryan and Seth he was born and raised in Vegas and often made donations to the fertility clinic with his buddies to pick up spare drinking money.

Seth's eyes were bugging out more than usual. "Really? You didn't have money to drink?"

"This was before my parents convinced me to go to law school. I was always floating between jobs. The one that lasted the longest was a telemarketing gig I picked up. Kept that one four months. Since my first day in court as a defense attorney, I've only taken three vacations, and those were because my wife told me if I didn't, she was going to leave me. Guess I've become a workaholic. Hated to take a break to come out here, but how many chances do you get to find out you have a son? Got three girls at home, and damn it, I'd love to have a son, even if you didn't take my name." Will took a sip of his margarita and looked around for the restroom. When he spotted it, he told them he'd be right back.

Just as the door to the men's room swung shut, "Diamond Dave" Diamond strolled into Boa and scanned the room. It took him less than ten seconds to spot Ryan and Seth, and as he jangled his way across the room, heads turned. He was wearing a red Elvis jumpsuit covered with bangles, beads, and brocade, unbuttoned to the waist.

"Boys!" he hollered, sliding into the booth beside Ryan, giving him a sideways hug, glancing at the pitcher of margaritas. "What are those? Sissy drinks?"

Seth cringed and looked like he wanted to slide under the table.

Ryan moved toward the center of the booth so he could get a better look at Diamond Dave, who seemed to be pushing sixty. He looked enough like Elvis, but his eyes seemed set too far apart and his hair appeared hopelessly thin.

Dave noticed his gaze and felt the top of his head. "Used to have more. Not like you or Elvis, but enough. Thirty years doing this is enough to make any guy bald."

Will made it back from the restroom and introduced himself to Diamond Dave. They ordered forty-day, dry-aged New York strip steaks and baked potatoes, and Dave had a bottle of bourbon brought to the table along with four shot glasses.

"A real man's drink," he proclaimed, clinking glasses so hard Seth's nearly spilled.

Diamond Dave was a frequent donor at the clinic throughout the seventies and eighties. "Keep churning out the good stuff even now. Clinic closed down, though. Some workout joint is there now."

"I know," Ryan told him. "I went there with my friends, hoping to meet Dr. Johns."

"Great guy," Diamond Dave said. "I wonder what he's doing now." He didn't allow anyone any conjecture and answered the question himself. "Getting a well-deserved rest, I'm sure. Come to think of it, don't know how many years I have left in me. Do you know how hard it is to shake, rattle, and roll once your hips and knees start to revolt?"

Ryan and Seth laughed.

"So," Will said. "What next?"

Ryan pulled two cards out of his wallet. "Seth found a DNA testing lab, and I was hoping you guys might provide samples to see of either of you are a match for me."

"No problem," Will said. "We're great at giving samples, right, Dave?"

Dave was straight-faced. "I'm the best damn sample giver this country has ever seen."

61

The funeral parlor Nancy chose for Wendall was near his old clinic, with plenty of parking for the hundreds of friends and acquaintances wishing to pay final respect. Logan flew in the morning of the wake and headed directly there from the airport via taxi. He got out, paid the driver, and stared at the white-columned, formidable building before he dared to enter.

He had missed saying good-bye to his uncle in person. Nancy said that Wendall was hanging in there and she thought there was still time before she needed to pull Logan away from his job, but she couldn't have been more wrong. Had she been in denial? Had she not been able to admit the end was so close at hand?

Logan spotted Nancy near his uncle's casket in the field of floral offerings covering the wine-colored carpet. With her graceful neck and good posture, she looked like Grace Kelly in an outfit at odds with her personality. The black dress she wore was long with a high collar, long sleeves, and cuffs—a straitjacket confining her body but unable to stem the tide of her unwieldy grief.

Logan walked along the wall, wearing his rumpled suit for the third time that month, nodding at the men he recognized—Wendall's golf buddies and poker pals who had been to the home. When he made it to Nancy, he lightly touched her linen sleeve. She turned and fell against him, a painful wail rising as she buried her face in his last clean dress shirt. He envied her the ability to let her feelings out. He felt numb and cold, in shock, going through the motions. Together, they stood over Wendall in his elegant split-lid mahogany casket and gazed at him. He wore a silvery suit with a white dress shirt, opened at the collar. To Logan, he appeared gaunt, a wasted figure that couldn't be the Uncle Coconuts who had played ball. *I do not like this thing called death,* he thought. *It erases everything as if it never happened, as if it were a dream.*

Nancy cupped Logan's bent elbow and steered him to a hallway, away from the group of mourners. She found a bench and sat him down, but she remained standing perfectly still in her ghastly dress, a dress that wasn't her at all, but neither did this day become her. She reached out to smooth the lapel on the rumpled suit she'd picked out with him so many years ago. "There's something I've got to tell you."

Her voice was serious, quiet, intent. She had his complete attention.

"Your uncle said something right before he passed, something he wanted me to tell you. He said he knows that you know, and it's okay, that sometimes rules need to be broken. And you have his permission to break this rule this one time. Because..." she struggled to recall Wendall's exact phrasing, "these are special circumstances."

Logan closed his eyes and remembered the night he met Ryan Wyatt at his uncle's home in Vegas with incredible vividness. He remembered late that night, when he couldn't sleep, when he crept downstairs, barefoot. He could still see the dim kitchen, illuminated only by the stove light, and he could see around the corner into the living room. He could still see Uncle Wendall burying a folder beneath old newspapers, and he could see how intent the good doctor was on hiding that paperwork and having its contents burned.

He recalled sneaking back upstairs, the floorboards silent, never betraying his footfalls as he climbed the sweeping staircase. He had tiptoed down the hallway and crawled back into bed, Elvis still playing on the stereo like he'd never left his room. But when Uncle Wendall stood by his open doorway and watched him feign sleep, Logan had to wonder if, for a split second, out of the corner of his eye, Uncle Wendall saw him peer around the corner into the living room, knew he saw him bury the folder in the burn pile, and realized he would come back and uncover the truth.

He must have. Wendall had known all these years that his nephew, his boy, and, to the core of his being, really his own child—for he had been there every step of Logan's journey since the boy's life had been destroyed—knew, and it was okay.

For once, the rules didn't apply. Though only the shell of Uncle Wendall remained, his spirit already having moved on to bigger and brighter things, he knew, in parting, the greatest gift he could give his boy was the exceptional news that his hero, his comfort, the luminary who sang him to sleep at night lived on in the form of a lad Logan's own age named Ryan, and he knew that Logan would tell that young man that his father was the King. And it was okay.

62

The next three weeks saw three more contestants eliminated, leaving Ryan, Seth, and two women left to vie for the *It Factor* crown. The more the judges complained that Ryan hadn't discovered his own identity or found his niche in the music industry, the more people at home voted for him to stay in the competition.

On a night when most of the cast and crew were already asleep, Ryan had the overwhelming urge to talk to Bea, but she wasn't answering her cell phone and wasn't on her computer to answer his instant messages. Ryan would have called the house but didn't want to wake her parents. It was well after midnight, and he and Seth had to be up early to choose which Beatles songs they'd sing on the next show.

Seth looked up from his laptop. "Don't forget we have to tape 'Going Home' segments this week."

"What's that?"

"Come here. I'll show you one from last year on YouTube."

Ryan pulled his desk chair over beside Seth's and sat.

Bethany Green, a contestant who looked like Betty Boop but talked like a trucker entered a gymnasium filled with students screaming her name and waving banners. The high school principal declared that this would be Bethany Green Day forevermore, and the mayor stepped forward to give her a hug and an oversized key to the city. After a drive through the streets of Minneapolis, Bethany and her parents arrived at a modest white clapboard house with a sagging porch. Bethany gave a tour of her room, where she showed off her archery trophies, and then joined her parents on the porch, where three overstuffed chintz-covered chairs had been placed so the three could chat and share fond memories of what Bethany was like as a child.

Ryan sighed. He did not look forward to going through that with his parents.

Seth was far from crestfallen by the prospect of returning to Austin, Texas, where his dad told him they had planned a big barbecue and parade in his honor.

"Hey, wait, I forgot to show you something." Seth entered a web address and a dozen thumbnails appeared alongside a Skype window.

Ryan sighed. "I didn't get to chat with Bea today. For some reason, I really feel like I need to talk to her."

"I know you miss her. Check this out." Seth's eyes darted around till he located where the volume control for the Skype window was and pointed at the screen. "I'm already logged in."

The handle "SethSings87" appeared in a box below the Skype window, where people were chatting. The site was called The Sixth Realm.

"You pay for credits and get live readings with psychics. I was thinking maybe you could ask a medium who your dad is."

Ryan sat up straighter. "Are these guys legit?"

"There are two thousand of them registered to give readings, and they're all over the world. Of course, they're not all logged on at the same time. And to answer your question, some are just card readers and some have their thumbs up their ass, but there are a few who are spot on with some really amazing stuff."

"Like what?"

"Okay, well, there's this medium named Redd Hansel. He's on TV in the UK. I went into a private reading with him and he described how my grandfather died, what he looked like, and some things about him no one would know."

Ryan's curiosity was piqued. "For instance?"

"My grandfather always liked to take out his wallet, pull out all his credit cards, and say, 'Look how many I've got.' It was a totally lame thing to do and we always laughed at him, but the point is, Redd said, 'Your grandfather is showing me his wallet and taking out charge cards and stacking them on the table. There's a whole pile of them. Does this mean anything to you?' My jaw hit the floor, I'm telling you. That is not something many people do. And there was other stuff too. Redd said, 'I see tractors around him. Oh, a lot of tractors.' My grandpa was a tractor dealer. How many of those do you know?"

Ryan was beginning to feel a sense of excitement. "Okay, I'll talk to this guy. Is he online now?"

Seth found Redd's thumbnail, clicked on it, and the screen widened, showing Redd at his computer, drinking from a huge mug. His face was plump and his eyes glittered from behind his round-framed glasses. His comb-over was sandy, and his smile was crooked. Ryan liked him at once.

In the conversation box, Seth typed *hello.*

"We can see him but he can't see us. We have to type our questions," Seth explained.

Recognizing Seth's user ID, Redd's voice boomed through the speaker.

"Hi, Seth. How are you?"

Good, Seth typed. *Is now a good time for a private?*

"You bet."

Seth clicked the on-screen button that said "private reading."

"I've got twenty-nine dollars in credits," he told Ryan. "That should be good for six or so minutes."

He bent over the keyboard and began to type to Redd. *I've got a friend here who doesn't know who his birth father is. Can your guides provide any information?*

"What's your friend's name and date of birth?"

Ryan Wyatt, Seth typed.

"October 3, 1988," Ryan said, and Seth entered that as well.

"I see a somewhat overweight gentleman with dark hair, and he's showing me his hands. He's wearing a lot of rings and looks a lot like Elvis Presley."

We think his dad might have been an Elvis impersonator because his mom received sperm from a bank in Las Vegas, Seth typed.

"Very possible," Redd said. The man I see has a large ego and some might consider him pious at times, yet he can also be very generous and charming. He's showing me a wardrobe full of jumpsuits. I definitely feel he's an entertainer and that many know his name and he is considered successful. But there is darkness around him and I'm seeing the symbol of a broken heart over his left shoulder. I usually see that when someone is divorced. There is also a sense of disconnection, a surreal feeling like he is not aware of his surroundings. I get that sometimes with drinkers."

"His name," Ryan whispered. "Can he tell us his name?"

Seth laughed. "You don't need to be quiet."

He typed the question Ryan asked.

Redd thought for a moment. "All I'm seeing is a flashing billboard with Elvis' name in lights. His dad must have really loved the King."

63

The Super Shuttle ride from LAX to Logan's apartment was uneventful, but when he arrived, his door was broken and his place was packed with detectives investigating a break-in that occurred while he was in Vegas.

Marilyn and Tom stood where Logan's bank of computers had been and watched a technician dust for prints.

"You won't find anything," Marilyn told them.

Logan tried to contain his rising panic. His vial of Elvis' hair and his framed photo of his Siamese cat were no longer beneath his bedside lamp, which had been knocked over. He reached inside his jacket, pulled out his tablet, typed a note, and handed it to Tom. *What happened?*

Tom ran a hand through his hair and frowned. "There was a break-in last night. How they knew you were out of town is anyone's guess."

A detective brushed by Logan and stopped. "How who knew?"

Marilyn exploded. "I told you. People at *Flash* want me dead!"

The third detective in Logan's tiny apartment stepped forward. He had a pad out and his nametag read "Det. Hume." "People at *Flash*, you say? Anyone in particular?"

Marilyn couldn't keep her voice down. "Cecil Bertrand, who's probably taking orders from Alastair Neville, who's disappointed I didn't like to sleep with him whenever he flew in from England. You do know I was raped, beaten, and left for dead in a Venice motel room, right? They do tell you guys these things, right? Not that anyone was caught or charged, because you were probably bought off."

Detective Hume looked at her like she was crazy and wrote something on his pad. Logan could see it from where he stood. He'd written "Bertrand" and *"Flash"* down in black ink at an angle, ignoring the blue rule-lines on the page.

Tom had his arm around Marilyn as he moved her to Logan's bed and sat her down on the edge of the now-bare mattress. The blanket and sheet were in a pile on the floor, and the pillowcase had been removed from the pillow before it was slit, scattering white snowy clumps of polyester fiberfill around the room.

Detective Hume looked at Logan. "This your place? How long were you gone?"

Logan held his hand out to Tom, who gave him back his iPad. He typed his answer while Hume looked at Tom, puzzled.

"He doesn't talk," Tom explained, turning to Marilyn. "And no one's going to get you. Anywhere you need to go, I'll be with you, and they do *not* want to mess with me."

"What if there are four of them? An entire gang of guys with guns?"

Tom shook his head. Trying to reassure her was pointless, so he turned his thoughts to security. "I knew Logan's door was flimsy. He should have had a better door. And better locks. And an alarm."

Hume read Logan's note aloud. "Gone overnight. Left yesterday morning. Uncle's funeral in Vegas." He handed the iPad back to Logan and wrote something down. The other detectives were done dusting for prints and taking photos. They joined Hume and the three detectives stood there, looking cramped in the tight quarters.

The New Elvis

Marilyn rose and took a step toward them. "Do you know a guy with the LAPD named Allan Griffin? He's not with the CHP, but he chased me down while I was on the freeway and planted a tracking device on my car."

"We're Hollywood, Ms. Coffey," the shortest detective, whose name was Fraser, said.

Marilyn was incredulous. "So you never mix it up between divisions?"

"Do you have the device?" the middle detective, named Lauder, asked.

"No, but my friends said it was was definitely official."

"And what would constitute a *definitely official* tracking device?"

Marilyn was distraught. "Some kind of number on it."

Detective Fraser's voice was heavy with sarcasm. "Why don't you bring it by the department and have us take a look-see?"

Marilyn was ready to punch the wall, but Tom grabbed her and held her tight. Logan crossed the room and sat at the top of his bed, where his pillow had rested. He looked down between the bed and the table, and felt a flood of relief. The vial of Elvis' hair and the framed photo of Professor X had fallen on the floor. He could see the edges of both peeking out from beneath the bed.

"Anything down there?" Hume asked.

Logan sat up quickly and stared at him, an impassive look on his face.

Hume looked at the other two detectives and sighed. "We're done here."

"What are you gonna do about this?" Marilyn demanded.

Hume shrugged. "We'll run the prints we got and see if they match any in the system."

Her voice was shrill. "That's it?"

Detective Fraser stepped forward, still in a sarcastic mood. "Ms. Coffey, what would you like us to do?"

64

Ryan and Seth pored over the Beatles songbooks left in the music room. They had half an hour until the vocal coach arrived and then, depending on who worked out with the coach first, the other one would have additional time to choose which song to sing in the next show. The two women left in the competition had a different coach and were practicing next door. They could hear *Yesterday* faintly through the wall as Noelle sang it with heartfelt emotion.

Ryan turned to Seth.

"There's something Redd said that made me think. 'His dad must have really loved the King.' Past tense. Do you think my dad is dead?"

Seth thought about it for a moment, closed his buggy eyes and sighed. "Sometimes he sees people that are still alive, I think. Good mediums can see all sorts of things, past, present, future."

Ryan persisted, "But he said *loved*, not love."

Seth smoothed his dark blond wavy hair with his hands to flatten it down. "But when Redd did the reading on my grandfather, he described what he died from and how he crossed over, and he didn't go into that this time."

Someone knocked loudly on the door to the music room.

"Shit," Ryan cursed. "We haven't picked our songs."

Seth called out, "Come on in!"

A woman with such a short neck her head seemed to spring directly from her torso waddled in. She was dressed in an orange floral print cocktail dress that fell below her knees, and her carefully coiffed hair was a silvery ash. Her hazel eyes sparkled and her smile was warm. As Ryan and Seth watched her make her way across the room, her gaze seemed fixed on

Ryan. Seth gave him a sidelong glance and a half smile, as if to say, *it figures.*

"I'm Corinne Crowley," she said, grabbing at Ryan's hands, causing him to drop the Beatles songbook he was holding. "I'm the producer of *All Of Our Days.*"

"It's a daytime soap," Seth said.

"Yes," Corinne said, barely giving Seth a glance, "and my daughter is seriously infatuated with you. She has been begging me to put you on the show, and it just so happens, we need to complicate the Jennifer Flurry storyline by adding a new love interest, and you, my dear, are it."

Ryan started to speak, but she cut him off. "No need to audition and sweat it out. The part is already yours. You won't have to leave L.A. We tape in Studio City. You'll be asked to sign a six-month contract, and you'll be paid ten thousand a week to start."

"What about *It Factor*?" Seth asked.

"This is a contractual obligation too, so we'll expect him to show up at the studio as soon as he's done here." She studied Ryan a moment. "Well, maybe not immediately. If you need two days after the *It Factor* finale to rest up, that's fine."

Seth laughed and Ryan's cell phone rang.

He got up and had to squeeze out of the bubble of personal space Corinne had created so he could answer the call.

It was Bea's mother. She had found Bea in her room that morning, dead from an overdose of painkillers.

65

After the break-in at Logan's apartment, they repositioned Marilyn's couch so it was closer to the dining room area and brought in desks so he could move in upstairs. Now that Tom was sharing Marilyn's bed, the couch that used to be his sleeping spot was delegated to Logan, who washed his sheet and blanket, bought a new pillow, packed his stuff in shipping cartons, and crated it all up to his new domicile.

No current stories, photos, contact information or leads had been left on the computers before Logan left town for his uncle's funeral. Everything of importance had been Dropboxed to Peter Corcioni in Chicago. There were no external hard drives anywhere in Logan's apartment containing anything a rival could use. In that regard, they had been careful, but they were not prepared for the next onslaught.

The first thing Logan did after he logged onto his new computer upstairs was visit dailycelebrity.com, the website he maintained that offered tidbits of gossip, photos from past issues, Marilyn's weekly blog, and a message board, where a host of alarming messages had been posted from visitors within the past seventy-two hours.

"What happened to *Daily Celebrity's* official fan page on Facebook? It's got to be a joke," a regular visitor commented.

"That photo of Marilyn is disturbing. Why would you post it?" asked another.

"Not pretty, guys," said a third.

Logan went to Facebook but couldn't log into the *Daily Celebrity* account. He went to his Logan Lockhart account instead, typed *Daily Celebrity* in the find window, and saw what the readers were talking about. The banner across the top of the *DC* account, which had been a panoramic shot of the Hollywood sign, had been replaced by words in 36-point typeface that screamed, "Marilyn Coffey is a lousy tabloid reporter. She's much better at other things!" The profile picture of Marilyn, shown back in her glam platinum days, was gone as well, replaced by a picture of a toilet that hadn't been flushed.

Logan found Tom in the kitchen, stirring honey into his tea. Logan waved at him, and Tom followed him back to the computer in the living room, where the *DC* Facebook page was displayed on the monitor.

Tom sat down heavily in Logan's chair and composed his thoughts before sharing them. "I've seen Facebook accounts hacked before. It's a pain in the ass getting things straightened out, but I know someone who can trace the IP of whoever cracked the password and changed it. Is the website still secure?"

Logan nodded and Tom got up.

Marilyn wandered out from the bedroom, where she'd been on the phone, and noticed their irritated expressions. "What's wrong?"

Tom shot Logan a warning look. "Nothing."

He headed back toward the kitchen and Marilyn padded after him in the new bunny slippers he'd bought her. "You want some tea? I just made some."

"You know better than to ask. Only coffee for Coffey."

"I was just being polite."

Marilyn had encouraged Logan to rehang his Elvis art upstairs, so he had filled the living room walls with his collection. Now he looked across the room at his Chris Consani art print entitled *Legendary Crossroads*, a black and white with spot color composition of Elvis seated on the bumper of a car Marilyn Monroe was leaning against, listening to him sing and play guitar. It wasn't as famous as Consani's *Java Dreams* of James Dean, Elvis Presley, Marilyn Monroe, and Humphrey Bogart at a bar, but *Legendary Crossroads* was Tom and Marilyn's favorite piece in Logan's collection.

Marilyn and Tom entered the living room with their cups of coffee and tea. Before they reached the couch, Tom was ready to play his guessing game again.

"Which story is true? One, Dena Newton hides in a large suitcase backstage after performances to avoid her fans. Two, Lisa Pollack keeps a collection of her taxidermied pets at home.

Three, Josh Guthrie has no testicles as a result of a hunting accident he had in Africa while shooting *Savannah at Sunrise*."

Marilyn sat down on the couch that was now Logan's bed.

"Three is true, and it's gross." She picked up the TV remote and began flipping through channels, stopping when she got to *It Factor*. "Oh, this is home week. I *adore* home week."

Tom moved Logan's new pillow and joined her on the couch. "What's home week?"

Marilyn sipped her coffee. "That's where the top four contestants return to their hometowns to see their families and fans. It's good stuff."

Logan looked up from his monitor. Ryan Wyatt was on the screen, wearing the blue scarf Bea had finished knitting for him. His father, identified on screen as Eugene Wyatt, sat to his left, and his mother, identified as Zella Stuart Wyatt, sat on his right.

Ryan was openly crying and his eyes were bloodshot.

"I guess the worst thing that's happened this year is that we lost Ryan's dear friend Bea Edwin," Zella said, her hands folded in her lap.

"This is the scarf she made me," Ryan told the audience, looking down at it, then back at the camera.

Logan thought he would stop breathing. His hands froze on the keyboard and he stared at his fingers. He went back in time to when he'd met her at Uncle Wendall's home in Vegas, and he could still picture her with her glorious blonde curls, standing only a few feet into the foyer area. Professor X was circling their legs, and he watched as Bea slowly lowered herself down so she could see him better. She had looked up at Logan and told him his cat was beautiful and even bothered to ask his name. He remembered her as she'd looked at Bar Fifty-Six that night, when Ryan was surprised they all wanted him to sing and she had laughed and said that was why they were there. Blinking back tears, Logan looked back at the TV screen, but seeing Ryan so grief-stricken made him feel worse.

"She had Rheumatoid Arthritis and then developed neuropathy," Zella explained. "It got so bad, she lost feeling in her feet and legs. She was taking so many different drugs, it was hard to keep track. Her mom found her in her room. She died of an accidental overdose. Or maybe she mixed the wrong things." She looked at Ryan. "Was that ever made clear?"

Ryan shook his head and wiped his wet face with the heels of his hands. Zella squeezed Ryan's shoulder. The trio onscreen faded as a montage of photos of little Bea and Ryan performing together onstage in school productions over the years filled the screen.

Logan got up from his seat and started to leave the room.

Marilyn looked over. "I'm sorry, Logan. Is the show too loud?"

Tom was still glued to the screen. "Damn, that kid looks just like a young Elvis."

66

The weeks passed, and working non-stop since his return from Uncle Wendall's funeral in Vegas while adjusting to sharing space with Marilyn and Tom had taken its toll. Logan needed a day off to clear his mind and think.

The evening he made the decision to ask for some "me" time, Marilyn was preparing a Mexican feast in the kitchen under Tom's direction. On top of his other stellar qualities, from the time he was old enough to hold a spoon until he left home at the age of eighteen, Tom had taken cooking lessons from his family's personal chef. Dan and Ron had been invited to join them that night, and when Tom opened the door, the ferret cousins entered, bearing gifts of wine.

Dan handed Marilyn the white and Ron gave the red to Tom before they plopped down on the couch without moving Logan's pillow and kicked off their shoes like they were finally home after a hard day's work.

Marilyn raised her eyebrows and stared at their socked feet. "You can move in next Tuesday."

"Dinner is served," Tom announced.

Dan groaned. "We're just getting settled."

Ron got up. "No problem. I'm starving."

A big bowl of guacamole had replaced the fruit bowl in the center of the table. It was too large to pass, so they took turns leaning in to scoop spoonfuls. With the cousins' arrival, the energy in the room was heightened. Tacos, Mexican bean salad, sweet corn tomalito, steak quesadillas, chicken enchiladas, and chiles rellenos were piled high on serving platters that Tom started passing counterclockwise. Logan filled his plate with two pie-shaped slices of quesadilla and a pile of salad. After everyone had something to eat, Tom poured the wine.

Ron threw a forkful of bright yellow tomalito into his mouth. "So we were at the Hollywood North Mall because Dan needed new sunglasses. We wanted to go to SunEyes, but Ron wanted to stop first at the bookstore for the new Richard Kadrey."

Marilyn took a sip of wine. "Oh, my God. I loved *Sandman Slim*."

Dan was busy picking the chicken out of his enchiladas, eating only the shredded bits of tender poultry. "So, we go into the bookstore and they're decorating the front window with clear globes and it's all beautiful and trendy, and we're in there when we hear a bunch of pops out in the hallway."

Ron put down his fork and took a gulp of red wine. "We thought they were fireworks."

Dan pushed the enchiladas aside and poked a relleno with his knife. "Someone was shooting up the mall. People started running out the emergency exit, but we stayed put with the managers."

"A mom and pop team," Ron interjected.

"The gunman came in and took the four of us to the back, but then he had us guys go up front and form a barricade while he held onto the lady."

Ron wiped his mouth. "We did a phony job of securing the front, obviously. Then he had us all sit in the back room."

Marilyn put more salad on her plate. "I can't believe you're even here after that. Did this make the news? Was the gunman insane?"

Dan swirled the wine in his glass and took another sip. "Definitely. And he had his rifle pointed at Joe."

"Joe owns the bookstore with his wife. He was in Iraq," Ron told them.

"The gunman called 911 and wanted to talk to a specific detective," Dan continued. "I guess he wanted to settle some score with him. Then he hung up and called his girlfriend and said good-bye."

Ron took over. "And then they turned off the electricity in the building, and when the gunman looked out to see what was going on, Joe jumped up, tackled him, and told us to grab the guns."

"Did you get photos?"

Dan sat up straighter and nodded. "You've got to seize the moment."

Marilyn glanced at Logan, who was lost in thought at how brave they'd been.

"Hey, anyone home?"

Logan blinked twice, then looked at Marilyn. The last thing Dan had said struck him harder than a Roger Clemens fastball. He took out his iPad and typed a note.

"Can you have tomorrow off?" she asked, after she read it.

Everyone at the table laughed.

"We gave him a great idea," Ron said, "and he's going to hit the streets Bronson style, dishing out some serious vigilante justice."

"No, really, what do you need to go do?" Dan asked Logan.

"Leave him alone," Marilyn admonished. "That's his business."

Logan smiled, took his iPad back, and picked up his forkful of quesadilla.

67

He had to do it today. He couldn't wait any longer. *Seize the moment.*

Online sources said that after *It Factor* wrapped, Ryan was going to be introduced as a new character on *All Of My Days*, playing the new kid in Suddenville, and as luck would have it, it taped in Los Angeles instead of New York.

Logan left early, before Tom and Marilyn rose, and drove to KBC in Studio City. It was a Monday, and the lot outside Stage 4 was filled with fancy rides lined up behind a tall, wrought iron fence too high to climb. Logan waited at the curb and watched as some of the stars filtered out of the building and went to lunch in groups of two, four, and six around noon. As the gate opened to let them out, Logan entered the lot on foot and headed to an open door large enough to accommodate enormous backdrops and scenery.

He stepped into another world, a brightly lit beach. White sand covered the floor of the sound stage, and towels, umbrellas, and a lifeguard tower added realism. The backdrop was a green screen. They would fill in the ocean later.

Ryan sat by himself, opening a Styrofoam carton containing cold spaghetti and meatballs, a wedge of garlic bread, and a stub of corn on the cob. He wore a dark Speedo and classic Vans that were black with a wavy white stripe and white laces. As Logan approached, he bit into the corncob and squinted, trying to place him.

Logan pulled out his iPad and it clicked for him who he was. "Hey!" he cried.

A man wearing denim overalls rushed over. "Everything okay here?"

Logan was six yards away.

Ryan shooed the man away. "It's cool. This is someone I know from a long time ago."

The man looked dubious but headed off.

"Pull up a chair," Ryan told Logan.

Logan looked around. There was a group of folded canvas chairs by the wall. He set his iPad down on a closed trunk, unfolded a chair, brought it over, sat down beside Ryan, and then jumped up to retrieve his iPad.

Ryan put his corn down and picked up his garlic bread. "You hungry?"

Logan shook his head.

"So, how you been?"

Logan typed a note and passed it to him. Ryan read it and then studied Logan carefully. "You have something important to tell me?"

He held onto the tablet, out of Logan's reach. "You watch this show?" He waved at the beach set with his bread in a gesture of dismissal. "It's crap. And the girl I'm supposed to be in love with is a brat. Don't even like her. Don't even know how I do it."

Logan's eyes were on the iPad.

"We're done at five," Ryan said finally. "If you have something to tell me, you're can tell me then. You're not going to write notes and pass 'em to me like we're in fourth grade. I know you can talk. I called your uncle a week after we met to see if he might reconsider telling me who my father is. I tried every ploy I could think of to get him to spill, but he wouldn't. So then I asked him about you. He said you could talk if you wanted to, but something scared you so badly, you think you can't. But you can, you know? You can do anything you want. And if you do write a note to me, I'm not gonna read it." He squinted up at the clock on the wall. "I guess that gives you less than five hours to find your voice."

His speech completed, he handed Ryan back his iPad and left the set to finish his lunch in another room.

68

On the way to Ryan's Studio City apartment, Ryan stopped at a liquor store and came out with a large yellow box that he placed in Logan's lap inside the agate grey metallic Porsche Boxster convertible he now drove. Logan studied the box as Ryan navigated the car through pretty streets and byways. An anchor and life preserver logo was placed next to the brand name, Cerveza Pacifico Clara, imported beer from Mazatlan, Mexico, and there were a dozen twelve-ounce bottles in the box. Ryan was now dressed in a white pullover, jeans, and the same sneakers he wore on set. Next to him, Logan felt pale and shabby in his skinny jeans and pilled green sweater. Was this a box of liquid courage that would help him find his voice?

"I haven't bought a house yet," Ryan explained as they approached a sprawling three-story apartment complex that stretched down the block. Once inside the security gates, they headed down a winding path through gardens and picnic areas with barbecues. Logan counted three swimming pools and four hot tubs by the time they made it to Building 11.

They took the elevator to the third floor, got off, and walked to the last unit on the right. There, Ryan pulled out his keychain, which had a picture of Bea in Lucite attached to it. "My girl," he said, holding it up so Logan could see her bright eyes, her blond curls, and her perfect white teeth. "You remember her. In better days."

The key went into the lock and Ryan let Logan enter the apartment first. No bachelor pad, this place. Ryan had appointed a decorator to bathe the place in black and blue, with red used as an accent color. The playpen-style seating in the living room was clustered around a square, double-glass-topped oak table. Beneath the glass, pictures of Ryan and Bea were grouped with pairs of movie ticket stubs.

"Have a seat anywhere," Ryan said, pointing toward the living room. He took the box from Logan and disappeared around a corner. Logan tried to figure out where to sit. Ultimately, he chose a spot opposite a wall that had a full color portrait of Ryan and Bea on it. The picture was taken in a backyard. They sat on the lawn, and a big black Newfoundland was wedged between them, its tongue lolling.

Ryan came back and handed him an open bottle of beer. "Drink. And then we're gonna work on your windpipe."

Even though Logan had never been to Ryan's apartment, he felt at home and completely comfortable. He also felt calm. Calm that the news he had to share would come out in this safe place, this warm home Ryan had created for himself.

Ryan took his Vans off and put his feet up on the couch. Leaning back against a red pillow the shade of ripe cherries, he studied Logan. "Do you ever drink?"

Logan shook his head.

"Have you ever even tasted alcohol?"

Again, Logan shook his head.

"Man, I get the feeling you've missed out on a lot," Ryan said. "So, what happened to you?"

Logan closed his eyes and relived the fateful night. He watched as his father's car entered the block and a mustard-colored sedan careened around the corner and rammed his father's Chevelle into the curb. A grimy white car coming from the opposite direction roared past him and rammed the Chevelle's front bumper. He watched as his father and the men leapt from their cars. He heard the gunshots and watched his father collapse like a dropped marionette behind his open car door. He heard himself scream and saw the killers' heads turn. He heard one of them shout, "Get the kid!" He was running as fast as his legs would take him, through his gate, through the backyard to the spot where a gully had been dug beneath the fence. He pushed the Elvis album into the Henns' yard first and then shimmied his way under the chain-link to safety. He hid behind the Henns' large tree with the album clutched against his small, quaking body. The men were in his yard, stumbling and crashing through the clutter. He held his breath, afraid to make a sound. An explosion of sirens rose and wailed like the cries of fallen angels. The angry men hesitated. The one killer told the other that they had to go, but the other one argued against it and said, "We gotta get the kid! He saw us!" They continued to argue. The less aggressive of the two told his friend, "He doesn't know what he saw," but the first man was hard to convince. They continued to argue as they fled, and both their cars were gone when he finally gathered the courage to head back out to the street. He tried to reason with himself. The killers were gone now. He had never tried to identify them, and they must know that, because no one had found them. At some point over the years, they realized he either didn't know what he saw or was too afraid to say anything. He had been afraid, but he had taken it too far. Not only would he not say anything to the police about the killers, he wouldn't say anything, period.

 Ryan let his question to Logan go. "So, Bea died while I was on *It Factor*. Oh, my God, what a show. The judges kept comparing me to Elvis. Any song I sang, they told me that's how Elvis would have sounded if he sang it. They wanted me to find my own voice. But I've never copied Elvis. I've been me all along." He took a sip of beer. "Bea was found dead in her bedroom by her mom the week the show was down to the top four. I made it that far, likely as a result of all the people out there who still love Elvis, you know? And then we did home week, and I was still raw. I kept telling Bea to watch what she was taking, but her legs got funny. She couldn't even feel 'em. She was in bed all the time. She was depressed even when I was there with her. She didn't want a wheelchair, but I was working on her to get one. Told her I wouldn't mind pushing her around. I told her I'd already been pushing her around for years anyway." He paused. "That's a joke. She had me wrapped around her little finger." He glanced up at the photo Logan was studying. "That's us, in my old backyard. And that's Nana. She's gone too. She was a good dog." He finished his beer and set the empty bottle on the glass-topped table. "You want another beer?"

Logan still had half a bottle but was feeling the beer's effects. He hadn't eaten, and Ryan seemed to sense it.

"You want something to eat? I'll get us something to eat."

Ryan left the room and Logan looked outside. The sky was as blue as a dyed Easter egg, and someone on a balcony across the way was trying to fly a kite, thrusting it out and reeling it in, trying to get the wind to catch it.

The plates Ryan carried to the table were filled with roast beef sandwiches cut into squares next to mounds of potato chips. He put a plate in front of Logan and then put one in front of himself before he took a swig of his second beer.

"Bea and I, we tried for a long time to figure out who my dad is. My friend on *It Factor*, Seth, has a close friend who works in a DNA testing lab. I issued an invite on the show for anyone who donated sperm at your uncle's fertility clinic about twenty or so years ago in Vegas to contact me, and we met two guys at a steakhouse—a serious lawyer type from Colorado and an Elvis impersonator who was a little long in the tooth and over-the-top gaudy. Neither of those guys were a match, but I think they were more disappointed than I was. Then Seth turned me on to this online psychic who gave me the impression that my dad might be an Elvis impersonator, but he talked about him in past tense, like he's dead now."

Ryan bit into a square of sandwich, washed it down with beer, and abruptly changed topics. "Hey, you play Call of Duty? I've got it in the other room. You ever go online and play?"

Logan shook his head and took another tiny sip of beer. He wondered if Ryan felt isolated. Again, Ryan seemed to sense his thoughts. "Yeah, it's a little lonely here. Studio City is way different than Beverly Hills. Not better, not worse, just different. When you're on a show, it's hard to make friends. The actors hang out sometimes, but they're an odd lot, all trying to climb over each other to get out of daytime and into prime time. And girls just want to hook up with you to say they did. It's not a good scene."

Logan remembered he still had his uncle's Mass card in his wallet. He pulled it out and showed it to Ryan, who took a moment to realize what it was. "Holy shit. Your uncle died about two months ago?"

Logan nodded and closed his eyes. Ryan was telling him how sorry he was but Logan was transported to another scene in his mind.

Uncle Wendall was behind the wheel of his Cadillac, making the drive back to Vegas at what seemed to be a slug's pace. Little Logan stared out the window at the arid desert scenery and wondered where all the buildings were. In the early evening light, he looked down at *Elvis' Christmas Album*, the only thing he wanted to bring aside from some ragged clothes and shoes. He felt Uncle Wendall's eyes on him, but when he snuck a look back, Uncle Wendall looked away and began to sing the song he'd taught him long ago. *This old man, he played one, he played knick-knack on my thumb, with a knick-knack paddy-whack, give a dog a bone, this old man came rolling home.*

Logan squirmed and Uncle Wendall intuited he needed to go to the bathroom.

In as long as it takes for a song to play on the radio and another one to begin, they were at the rest stop. Relief washed over Logan. Uncle Wendall cared about his needs. He walked around to the passenger side of his big blueberry Cadillac and Logan caught a whiff of his tropical cologne. *Uncle Coconuts.*

"You going to stare at that album all night or are you gonna come with me?"

Logan looked up. Uncle Wendall had withered and grayed.

He looked down at his own legs but they were now clad in skinny jeans, and the Elvis album was on the dashboard.

He looked back up at his fragile, aged uncle.

"It's time," Uncle Wendall said.

"For what?" Logan asked, knowing full well it had nothing to do with making use of the rest stop.

Uncle Wendall stood at the open passenger door and waited for Logan to understand.

"I know you said I could tell Ryan the truth, but he wants me to *tell* him."

The old man turned his rheumy gaze up to the heavens. The stars were beginning to glint like sequins on the fabric of darkening sky and the air was still.

"You are safe. I am watching over you now. You can speak. All you need to do is try."

Logan opened his eyes and looked across the coffee table at Ryan, who had been talking about loss. "Grief counseling," he said. "It's really helped me, listening to other people talk about about they're going through. I attend a group that meets three times a week and I've already processed some stuff. I've cried a whole lot too and wonder when I'm going to stop. I think groups are better than one-on-one therapy because there's a different dynamic. Everyone starts out as strangers, but you become friends pretty quick. I guess you have to, when you're bawling your eyes out in front of them."

Logan took another sip of beer and Ryan broke into a lopsided grin. He sat up straight and leaned toward him. "Finish the bottle."

Logan obliged, and a burp erupted, surprising them both.

Ryan jumped up. "Oh, my God! Your first word is *burp*!"

Logan was so startled he felt dizzy and saw sparks dancing in his field of vision.

Ryan ran over to where Logan was sitting and put his arm around him. "Maybe I can try some pre-performance stuff on you to get you to loosen up. Go ahead and try to cough. Take a deep breath and then push the air out of your lungs in a blast."

Logan honked, and they both started laughing. Then Logan gasped. His honk of a laugh sounded like rusty hinges on a Radio Flyer wagon being scraped across metal.

Ryan was elated. "You need more to drink." He ran out of the room and returned with another beer, which Logan drank in big gulps.

He felt faint but excited and ready to try again.

"Say A, E, I, O, U," Ryan instructed, so close to Logan on the dark blue couch, he was nearly on top of him, ready to shake the vowels out of him.

Logan croaked like a frog. "A, E, I, O, U."

They looked at each other, eyes wide.

"Okay," Ryan said. "Now tell me what you wanted to tell me."

He sat back against the cushions, expectant, and waited.

Logan cleared his throat and sounded like a person with bronchitis trying to dredge up phlegm. He took another sip of beer. His voice might be hoarse and he might sound peculiar but his real voice would come back with practice. The important thing was that Ryan heard him. He scooted back on the couch so he could face Ryan fully and took a deep breath.

"Elvis is your father," he said, daring to speak the words he'd written a thousand times in letters never sent.

Ryan looked at him, completely blank. "You mean my dad is an Elvis impersonator. I know, man. I always suspected it."

Logan shook his head emphatically, determined to make Ryan understand him. "The *real* Elvis. The *real* Elvis Presley. The *famous* Elvis Presley. *He's* your dad."

The tables had turned.

It was Ryan's turn to be speechless.

69

Because traffic was bad, it took a while for Ryan and Logan to make it back to the Logan's apartment complex in the Hollywood Hills. On the way, Logan explained how he had sold his graphic arts school graduation Caddy to win an online auction for clippings of Elvis' hair saved by Homer "Gil" Gilleland, the King's personal hairdresser, just in case he had the opportunity to test it with Ryan's.

Still in shock, Ryan mumbled something about DNA tests and followed him to Marilyn's apartment, allowing Logan to lead him inside.

"We're home," Logan croaked.

Marilyn dropped the bowl of watermelon she was carrying and pieces flew across the white carpet. Tom rushed in, saw the spilled fruit, saw Marilyn's astonished expression, saw Logan standing there with Ryan, and didn't know what to make of it. He dropped to his knees and began to pick the pieces out of the carpet, reaching up toward Marilyn to retrieve the tipped bowl she still held in her hand.

"Mare, what is it?"

"He—he talked."

Ryan and Logan laughed.

"Go on in," Logan told Ryan. "Take a seat on my bed. I mean, the couch. Jeez, I think I need some water."

Logan left Ryan with Marilyn and Tom and went into the kitchen.

Marilyn and Tom stared at Ryan.

"Hey, you're the kid from *It Factor*. You remember, Mare. The one who I said looked like Elvis." Tom went over to sit beside him. "I bet you get that a lot."

Before Ryan had time to reply, Logan returned with his water and sat down on the carpet to finish cleaning up the spilled watermelon.

"Oh, let me get a wet rag," Marilyn said. "I've got to scrub those spots out."

"Actually," Logan said, taking a sip of water and inspecting a square of watermelon like it was a precious gem, "there's a whole lot more to the story than you think." He felt his throat. "I think I've got to rest my voice. It's a little hoarse. You tell them, Ryan."

Marilyn returned from the kitchen and sat down on the carpet beside Logan. "How did you get your voice back?"

Logan pointed at Ryan, who leaned back into the cushions and looked around the room at Logan's Elvis artwork. "Actually, he had something important to tell me, and I told him he had to *tell* me if he wanted to tell me. As in, *speak.* And I guess it was important enough that he did."

Marilyn put her hand on Logan's arm. "What did you need to say?"

"Well, to start at the beginning, I'll have to take you back to when I found out I was a sperm donor baby," Ryan said.

Marilyn put the rag down and listened.

"I had just gotten back with my girlfriend Bea after years apart due to *my* stupidity when my dad called to say my grandparents were in town. I'd never met them because they retired to Thailand before I was born. It was typical and awkward, with them going through my baby album and whatnot. They started to discuss who I looked like and agreed I looked like my mom, but then my Grandma Katherine said something to the effect, 'Of course Ryan doesn't look like Gene,' and then my dad quickly interrupted her and tried to steer the conversation in a different direction. My mom left the room to check on dinner, and I followed her and asked her if my dad Gene was my real father. She put me off, and I got angry. Before I made it back to the living room, though, I overheard my dad talking to my grandparents and found out that my mom received a 'donation'—my grandmother's polite term—and that it happened in Vegas, she never found out who the father was, and that the doctor who helped her was named Wendall Johns, a guy who liked to keep things confidential.

"My girlfriend and I figured that since I looked so much like Elvis and my mom went to a fertility clinic in Vegas, there was a good chance my dad was an Elvis impersonator. We started watching tons of movies about Elvis, including documentaries done on impersonators, and tried to see if we could find him that way, and then we watched feature films where Elvis was played by an actor and tried to see if one of those guys might be my dad. One thing we thought was likely was that the guy could probably sing, since I can and my mom can't—at least, not very well.

"We put together a cover story for our parents, and Bea and I convinced our friend Noah to drive us to Vegas. I had found Dr. Johns' business address and phone number in a calendar my mom kept from 1988, the year I was born. The phone number had been transferred to someone new, so that left going to the fertility clinic and hopefully finding him. When we got there, we found out the clinic had turned into a tanning salon, but a neighbor told us we could find Dr. Johns in Rolling Hills Estates a few miles away. Once we got there, a neighbor pointed out his house, so we went to the door and rang the bell. Logan here answered the door and told us his uncle was out."

Tom was amazed. "Dr. Johns was your uncle?"

Logan nodded, and Ryan continued.

"We went to Bar Fifty-Six, a new lounge a block off the strip. They had a show featuring Elvis impersonators concentrating on the King's first big year, 1956, followed by karaoke. After that, we went back to Logan's house and met his uncle, who couldn't stop staring at me. We all thought he knew something, but he denied it, so we gave up and left."

Logan finished his glass of water and raised his hand. "I feel better. I can take it from here."

Ryan nodded and made a palms-out gesture to let him know the floor was his.

"That night, I listened to *Elvis' Christmas Album,* which I always did before I went to sleep. I must have still been full of adrenaline from going out, which I never did, and it was hard to get settled. I heard Uncle Wendall downstairs, and I snuck a peek into the living room. He buried a folder in a bin we kept next to the fireplace that we used to hold old papers to start fires with. I went back upstairs and waited to hear my uncle's bedroom door close. I waited, and then I went downstairs and dug the folder out of the pile. I found Ryan's mother's medical records and found a slip of paper with Elvis Presley's name on it with a number and the date, August 19, 1974.

"I knew Uncle Wendall kept matters confidential and never told clients who their babies' fathers were, and this case was no different. I took the slip of paper and left the folder with most of Ryan's mom's paperwork in the burn bin. After I graduated from graphic arts school and came here, I found out I could score some of Elvis' hair from the guy who used to cut it, so I sold my Caddy to pay for it."

Ryan interrupted. "Where is it? Can I see it?"

Logan got up, went to his desk, opened the top drawer, retrieved the bottle and the signed certificate of authenticity, and handed both to Ryan with all the reverence of a priest handling sacred items. Ryan glanced at the certificate and stared into the amber vial at the clump of dark hair. "I've got a friend named Seth who can have this tested against mine pronto."

Up on her knees, kneeling like she was in church, Marilyn gasped. "You're Elvis' biological son."

"Probably," Ryan and Logan said simultaneously.

70

The DNA test comparing Ryan's hair to a sample from the vial won at auction from Elvis' hairdresser confirmed paternity, and the day Logan's first story as a tabloid reporter came out, Tom booked the night of August 19th at the LVH for a blowout party.

The afternoon Marilyn and her crew joined Peter Corcioni and Ryan in the Tuscany Sky Villa marked the thirty-second year anniversary to the day Elvis called down to the front desk with a special request, and it was lost on none of them that the villa Tom picked for the party had encompassed Elvis' suite when the hotel remodeled and expanded it to a whopping 13,200 square feet in 1995.

Logan found the fireplace in the living room where Elvis' bed had once been and called Ryan over to see it. Like he once clutched *Elvis' Christmas Album*, Logan now held on to his issue of *DC*. The cover ran the headline, "Elvis has a son," and a photo of Elvis from the late fifties, dressed in a light blue, green, tan, and red striped shirt, a light blue cardigan, tan pants, and blue suede shoes, looking off to the left, faced the mirror image of Ryan, dressed nearly identically, looking off to the right. To celebrate, Ryan wore that same outfit today, but Logan stepped up his game, discarded his old suit, and wore a brand new tux that made him feel like royalty.

Tobias joined them. "Great story, man."

Ryan and Logan simultaneously said, "thanks," and they all laughed.

Tobias was in full beatnik garb, even wearing love beads. "I'm telling you, Logan, for your first story as a reporter, you don't mess around. It's better than any of mine, better than any of Dan's, better than any of Kevlar's."

Logan was amazed. "But you set the bar. It was your Helen Hester story that helped me to realize just how great a reporter you are. I worship you."

Tobias bowed down, his beads clacking against the studs on his vest. "You have surpassed me, sir."

Logan blushed and looked at the issue of *DC* again. He had to admit it was pretty good, but then again, he didn't have to go out and find the story. It had been with him all along and all he had needed was the opportunity to tell it.

Someone in the next room was clinking a glass to get everyone's attention. Tobias, Logan, and Ryan walked toward the sound and found Peter Corcioni standing on a chair, beating his water goblet mercilessly with his spoon, while Ron stood nearby, spotting him in case he wobbled.

Ryan looked around at the murals covering the ceiling and walls and felt like he was in Northern Italy.

"We initially tripled our production run, but we've sold out everywhere," Corcioni cried, slipping a bit and regaining his composure with Ron's help. "I'm in touch with the head of production back in Chicago. An investor in Nagoya wants us to translate the issue into Japanese and run a million copies exclusively for him. He's already wired the money, so it's a done deal. We brought in the top translators who are working on the copy now. And since his call, we've gotten similar requests from Germany, Australia, Italy, and the United Kingdom, so we're in the *big* money now, folks."

A cheer went up throughout the room.

Dressed in a heavily beaded aqua gown, Marilyn was beaming.

"Are you ready to go?" Tom asked her. He, like Logan, was in a tux.

Tobias came over. "I've let security know we're on our way."

Tom patted Tobias on the shoulder. "Good."

Marilyn bit her lip. "Are you sure we need it?"

Tobias rolled his eyes and Tom laughed.

"Mare," Tom said, "do you have any idea how many reporters are going to be at Bouchon at The Venetian to meet Ryan in person?"

"As many as can afford a fifty-dollar plate of French cuisine," Tobias quipped. "Unless you want the Grand Plateau, which is a lobster and sixteen oysters and ten mussels and eight shrimp and eight clams, plus crab when it's in season for a hundred and ten bucks."

Everyone stared at him.

"What? I checked the menu online. Tom booked exclusive use of the restaurant and courtyard. There's standing room for a hundred and fifty people and seating for half that number, if they want to eat with us."

"You know Cecil Bertrand's going to show," Pia said as she joined them, looking fabulous in a red gown slit up the side to her thigh. "Hell, even Alastair Neville might fly in from London."

Logan and Ryan came over and joined the circle.

Marilyn stared hard at the marble floor beneath her feet but her gaze wasn't focused. "And if he was mad at me before, he's going to be even angrier now."

Tobias gave her a hug. "Tom and I already thought of that. We gave pictures of everyone who still works at *Flash* to the security team we have in place at the restaurant. Anyone who makes a sudden move is going to be tackled from all sides. And everyone has to show a press pass, so that rules out the thugs who've already hurt you trying to slide in, because our guys know fake

ID when they see it. You know how airport security tightened up after 9/11 and the skies have been safe from terrorists since then? Homeland Security ain't got nothing on our team. They're the best. Trust us, Marilyn. Forewarned is forearmed."

"If those guys show up, they are *dead*," Tom said, and he looked like he meant it.

Marilyn thought about it. When she and Tom had asked Logan how he'd come to live with his uncle in Vegas and heard what he'd been through, they understood why he had stopped talking. Selective mutism had robbed him of a quality life for too long, and living in fear was no longer an option. If Logan could face the future with confidence, so could she.

As though Logan had read her mind, he approached her and took her hand.

"The past is the past. You've got to let it go."

She looked down at his hand, then into his eyes. "You've got a deal."

Fifteen minutes later, they were out in front of the LVH on South Paradise Road, climbing into stretch limos like it was something they did every day.

"You know I love you," Tom told Marilyn as he helped lift her gown so she wouldn't step on it as she got into their ride.

She turned to look back at him, her eyes glinting with good humor.

"How much do you think Alastair Neville would pay to sleep with me now?"

Made in the USA
Lexington, KY
04 March 2014